Tempted by the Bear

Book 1

Cover by Croco Designs
Editing by Jodi Henley and Red Adept Publishing

Tempted by the Bear

Book 1

V. VAUGHN

PART 1

CHAPTER 1

Annie

T HE DOUGH LANDS on the floured surface with enough force that a white cloud poofs up. I attack it with my hands to knead out excess air and give the bread texture. *That man!* That stunningly gorgeous beast of a man named Tristan De Rozier is going to be the death of me. He's a polar bear shifter who also happens to be my true mate. I lift the dough up, slam it down again, and give it a punch for good measure.

"Wow, who got you so worked up?" Carly asks as she enters the kitchen.

I glance over at my sister-in-law. Carly and her friend Sierra came to us less than a year ago to help save our clan. While she's my brother's true mate and a powerful alpha, she's also become my best friend.

"Three guesses, and the first two don't count."

"I don't understand why you don't give in to him." The coffee pot clatters as she removes it to pour herself a cup. "He's so hot, he might be the reason that glacier of his is melting."

I snort and push a strand of hair out of my face. "Let me count the ways. One, he's naked *all the time*. Do we really need to see that? Two, he taunts me as if I'm the one who's lovesick, when I know it has to be both ways. And three—" I sigh. I want to be courted. I want wine, roses, and adoration. "He takes such pleasure in embarrassing me." My throat tightens. "I hate it."

Carly's mug thumps on the counter, and she reaches out to stop my hands with hers. "You want romance and not little boy crush?"

I nod as I swallow down the urge to cry. "Is that so much to ask?"

"No. It's not. But men can be stupid when it comes to stuff like this."

"And if I give in, he'll think he can always treat me this way. So until he gets a clue, expect a lot of baking to happen."

The back door lets out a hollow echo as someone enters the mudroom that separates the kitchen from the outdoors. Within moments, the second door opens, which means the shifter who went out for a run is probably still nude. If that weren't enough of a clue, my body's slight hum of sexual tension confirms it. I don't look up as I say, "Good morning, Tristan."

But this man doesn't like to be ignored, and large hands land on the counter on either side of me as he whispers against the back of my neck. "Annie, love. You really should join me some morning."

He's smart enough not to press any body parts

against me, but my imagination has my blasted hormones reacting anyway. Joining Tristan as a bear would mean getting naked to shift with him, and I'm sure that's exactly what he wants. But he's never going to get it if he doesn't get a clue. I decide to take action. "Sorry, *love*, I need a little more than a boy who swings his dick around. We can talk when you become a man."

Tristan chuckles at me as my bold words bounce off his rock-hard body. He and his twin, Isabelle, have been houseguests for more than two weeks, and I've lost my patience. My face is flushed with shame, and my stomach churns, because I hate to lose my cool.

Carly's voice is dangerously close to her alpha tone when she says, "I wouldn't laugh if I were you. Annie doesn't get mad, but when she does, you better find a way to suck up quickly or you'll be eating garbage scraps."

Tristan has enough brain cells to remain quiet as he leaves, and I let out a big breath when Carly's hand lands on my shoulder. She turns me around for an embrace and says, "I'm sorry. You don't deserve this. Those stupid guiding spirits are supposed to be smart and give us what we need. Who the hell thought you should get a big oaf of a polar bear?"

"He is a big oaf, isn't he?"

"Not only that, but did you know his obsession with sweet potatoes is making his fur orange?"

"No!" My body shakes with an uncontrollable giggle.

"Yes, but don't tell him."

I squeeze Carly's arm. "Thank you. I don't know what

I'd do without you."

"You'll never have to know." She kisses my cheek and grabs her coffee cup to leave. "Can we have sweet potato fries for dinner tonight?"

"What a lovely idea."

I place the bread dough in a pan and set it on the fridge to rise.

The cutting board thunks down in the sink to be rinsed. But the aroma that floats to my nose tells me my blueberry muffins are done, and I abandon the dishes to remove them from the oven. I smile to myself when I use Sierra's trick of extending my claws and pulling out the muffin tin instead of using a potholder. It's funny how the brand-new werebears have taught this lifelong one a thing or two about our world.

The low rumble of my mother's car sounds in my super-sensitive ears, and I glance at the clock to discover she's early for our weekly business breakfast. I know why. She's anxious about the De Rozier clan assimilating into ours. While there are only twenty-five of them left, the two we're acquainted with are rather large forces that could disrupt our peaceful clan.

As if my thoughts call her, Isabelle, Tristan's twin, enters the kitchen. Her step is sluggish, and the cabinet clicks when I open it for ibuprofen before I greet her. I glance at her red-rimmed eyes and nearly-white hair piled on top of her head in a messy bun that probably caused pain to create. I ask, "Anyone I need to usher out before people get here?"

She shakes her head and winces at the motion. She holds out her hand, and I place two round tablets in her palm, and her voice is raspy when she says, "You really are an angel."

"Do you need a protein shake?"

"Yes, please. I promise I'll help you cook once it starts to work." Isabelle falls into a chair, and it creaks under her weight. She's the largest woman I've ever met. But that doesn't detract from her beauty. With her pale coloring, Nordic features, and sex appeal that rivals Sierra's, men want to climb her like she's Mount Everest. I expect if they get the chance, they're breathless when they hit the peak.

"No need. Carly should be down soon to help." Since my mother will want to talk out her issues about the De Roziers, I need Isabelle to leave us alone.

The whine of my blender is loud as my mother enters the kitchen. When it stops, I turn to greet her. "Good morning, Mom." Thick liquid pours into a glass, and I hand it to Isabelle.

Isabelle stands. "I'm going to go to my room until it's time for the meeting."

I watch as she shuffles out. Mom says, "Someone's enjoying civilization. I hear she's sampling the local delicacies too."

I frown, because I think Isabelle's party-girl attitude is masking something. "Don't you wonder why?"

"I do. While I'd like to welcome the De Rozier clan with open arms, I think it's wise to remember Polar Bear are known as the fiercest of our kind for a reason."

I try to imagine Tristan as a vicious bear. While the cocky attitude fits, his playful nature doesn't. But if he's the alpha and leading his clan to safety, he can't be all fun and games. *Huh.* I guess Isabelle isn't the only one hiding something.

CHAPTER 2

Annie

T HE BUZZ OF conversation and light-hearted joking makes me smile as I gaze at my family and friends seated at the large kitchen table. It's our weekly breakfast meeting to discuss the business of the Le Roux clan. Tristan and Isabelle have gone to town to give us privacy.

At the moment, peace blankets the kingdom, and only the core of our leadership needs to be present this morning. My brother, Brady, reaches past me to get more coffee. It splashes in his mug as he says, "Still torturing Tristan?"

I snort. "I wish. That man knows how to push buttons I didn't know I had."

"So what's holding you back?" He places a hand on my arm. "It's been three years, Annie. Kyle would want you to move on." Kyle was my husband and true mate. I recall his voice. So much has happened since he died, and the sound is fading in my memory. Now that Tristan has come along, the way Kyle's touch made me do more than hum with lust is distant as well. I blink back tears as the ache of my loss fills my heart. Kyle and my father died at the hands of our rival clan, the Veilleux.

"That's not the problem," I say. Amazingly, I've been graced with another true mate and with it the desire to love again. But. "I'm having a hard time accepting a man who angers me as if it's his goal in life."

Brady squeezes with a grip that reminds me of his power. "My wise sister once told me that communication is the key to a good relationship. You might want to try it."

I squint my eyes at him. "She'd never met Tristan."

A chuckle rumbles through my brother as he makes his way to the kitchen table to sit. I grab my mug and top it off as the aroma of coffee floats to my nose. I seat myself across from Ashton, the head of our warriors. I ask him, "How are Sierra and the babies?"

The ex-Navy SEAL smiles at me. "Couldn't be better. Lily has been fantastic about the whole thing." Ashton's wife, Sierra, was forced to have Victor Veilleux's children, and now that he's dead, his wife, Lily, is the leader of the Veilleux clan. She shares custody of Victor and Sierra's children, because one of the triplets will be the next Veilleux alpha.

I glance over at the empty seat where Keith, my brother's best friend, usually sits. The window behind it reveals a wintery landscape of stark white under the gray skies that hint of an incoming storm. Keith's in charge of our lumber business. His true mate died trying to rescue Sierra's children from the clutches of Victor less than a month ago, and he's struggling to get through each day. My mother catches my eye, and concern clouds her face. I guess she's thinking about Keith's sorrow too.

Brady says, "I'm glad to hear Lily is agreeable to the arrangement."

Carly says, "Me too. I think it means we can hope that the Veilleux will sit on our joint council." A few months ago, the third clan in the Northeast Kingdom, the Robichaux, agreed to join us in an attempt to keep peace and rule together. "Donna, you're like one of your grandchildren, squirming over there. Shall we move on to the subject of the De Roziers?" asks Carly.

My mother answers, "Yes. I have some serious concerns we need to discuss." She pauses for dramatic effect, and I refrain from rolling my eyes. "I don't think they're telling us everything."

Tristan and Isabelle came to stay as a mission to find a new place for their clan to reside. Being Polar Bear, they've suffered with the melting of the ice caps. In addition to poor leadership from their father, their numbers have dwindled. Because the majority of women in our clan are barren due to an ancient curse, we had hoped assimilating with the De Rozier bear would save us all.

"Me either," says Brady. He turns to Ashton. "I think it's time we saw what Tristan can do when it comes to fighting."

Carly nods. "Annie and I will work on Isabelle. She's trying awfully hard to find pleasure in vices. Something in my gut tells me drinking too much and hooking up isn't her usual behavior." She sips her coffee.

Mother holds her forkful of eggs midair and says, "I'll do some digging and see what I can find out. I have a friend in the Pacific Northwest who might know something. But this would be much easier if Annie would help us out." She swallows the bite as if she's gulping down my resolve.

All eyes turn to me, and I cringe. They want me to allow the true mate bond with Tristan to happen. "I'm sorry. Sex isn't something I'll do to take one for the team. Besides, don't you think Tristan will hide his secrets from me too?"

Carly is next to me and reaches for my hand. Her grip is warm as she says, "We want you to be happy first. You were lucky to find another true mate, and we both know it's meant to be. So what can we do to help you get comfortable with it?"

I gaze at the expectant faces. While almost two years ago we brought in four human women with werebear heritage to create the future generation, we only managed to secure the next alpha with Carly and Brady's children. The truth is, we do need more fertile females, and integrating with the De Rozier clan is a good way to make it happen. I swallow my pride. "Teach him how to treat women with respect."

Ash surprises me when he breaks out of his usual silence and says, "Consider it done."

I tilt my head at him but stop myself from asking

how. He may be quiet, but Ashton has an inner strength and honor that is volumes above most men. "Thank you." If anyone can turn Tristan around, I bet it's Ash.

CHAPTER 3

Isabelle

T HE POUNDING IN my head from my hangover has faded to a dull ache. I don't know what Annie puts in those protein shakes, but it always manages to cure me enough to where I can function. Wind flows through the open windows of the car Tristan and I borrowed as we drive to the Cat's Meow, a local cafe. The cold dances over my skin, and I wonder how we'll ever survive the warmer months in this climate. Polar bear run hotter than the black bear, and a Maine winter feels like summer to us.

Tristan says, "You're making me look like the responsible one. I might have to amp up my playboy and join you some night."

"Don't push your luck, brother. Annie may be okay with your bumbling act, but she'll never give in if you start sleeping around."

"Do you have any idea how hard it is to stay abstinent?" He lets out a low growl of desire and says, "Every time I lay eyes on Annie's curves, I want to—"

"Spare me the sordid details. You can hang on a little longer. I overheard Carly and Brady talking, and decisions are being made this morning. I bet we'll be discussing our arrangement soon."

"Patience never was my strong suit. But this plan is too good to screw up." Tristan shifts in his seat. "I'll manage."

I gaze out at the snow-covered pine trees. A sense of claustrophobia niggles at me, and I long for wide open spaces. I know moving here is good for the clan, because we really can't go on losing our numbers due to the dangers our melting ice poses. But I'm not sure how I'm going to find a way to love my new home.

I ask, "Do you think you can be happy here?"

Tristan slows to turn onto a road that is clear from snow. He cuts me a quick glance. "We haven't got much choice."

Home to me is nine months of daylight and three months of darkness, with temperatures that never rise above freezing. It also means very few people. As we get closer to the restaurant, I notice a fine-looking male on the sidewalk. I sense he's a werebear instantly, and that means he's fair game. A smile forms on my face. *Sweet redemption.*

Tristan chuckles as he pulls into the parking lot at the Cat's Meow. He heard my thoughts. He's the alpha of our clan, and if I don't remember to block my inner monologue, he hears me. "You're doing your best to sample every guy in town as if they're a box of chocolates, aren't you?" he asks.

"They're so easy, it's hard to resist." The door groans as I open it. Part of our deal will mean I'm going to provide Le Roux children to ensure the continuation of their clan. I'm practicing the fun part, because once I mate, it's supposed to be forever.

When we both get out and start to walk toward the café, Tristan says, "I don't think my dear Annie approves of your wanton ways."

"No. She doesn't, which is why I've stopped bringing them home." I wink at the guy coming toward us, and he flushes. I stop and turn to watch him after he's passed by. He glances over his shoulder and grins when I do. If I weren't with my brother and hungry, I'd do more than blow a kiss. No major loss. Chances are good I'll see him again. A woman my size isn't hard to find.

Tristan grabs my arm and pulls me toward the door. "I'm starving. Control yourself."

"On it. But have I mentioned how much I like a college town?" Yeah. Maybe I can be happy here.

When we get inside, I take in the surroundings. The tables are close together, and so many people are talking. But it's the odors that accost me. Polar bear have an extremely sensitive sense of smell, and I'm almost bowled over by the mix of food and human scents. A waiter walks by, and I focus on the aroma of pork sausage that makes my stomach growl.

A teeny attempt at a woman leads us to a table in the back. She's practically drooling over my brother as she stutters out her words. He flirts back, and I send him a warning glare. I'm pretty sure if this exchange got back to Annie, it wouldn't be a good thing.

When the girl leans in close to hand him a menu, Tristan leans forward to dazzle her. I give him the sister assist as I gush, "This place is darling. You should bring Annie here sometime."

The hostess's face falls, and I offer her a sympathetic smile. When she walks away, Tristan says, "Way to ruin my fun."

"Way to try to sabotage our plan." The plastic menu is slick in my hands as I lift it up to peruse the breakfast selections.

"Have a little faith, sister dear. Annie and I are true mates; nothing can come between us." He winks at me.

I smile back, but it's not quite real. My brother has always been the lucky one, and it's not fair that his true mate happens to be someone who can help him save our clan, even if it complicates things. Meanwhile, I'm testing out every male who makes my heart rate increase in the hopes of finding a true mate of my own. I sigh and decide to bury my woes in a large stack of blueberry pancakes.

After we place our order and our mugs are filled, Tristan sips his hot drink before he asks, "Which one do you think will tell me how to wise up around Annie?"

"Carly. Donna wants to, but she'll hold off for her daughter's sake."

"Not Brady? I find it hard to believe he lets his wife share alpha status so easily."

The concept of two alphas in a clan is fascinating. The fact that they're also married is mind boggling. How do they decide who's on top? "He seems to like her doing the female-assigned things in relationships."

Tristan nods. "Could be." His eyes light up, and he speaks in my head. *How much land do you think we'll get?*

My brother has a thing for power. The day he took over as alpha of our clan, he started to rule with dominance instead of the easy way of my father.

"I have no idea. But whatever it is, it won't be enough for you."

Tristan lets out a low growl before he says, "True words."

I grin, imagining his match with Annie. If her sexual restraint is any indication, she's going to counter my brother's need for control. Warm coffee fills my mouth as I drink from my cup. I may be the sacrificial lamb who has to bear children to save our clan, but Tristan's path isn't going to be the cakewalk he imagined. His true mate bond is going to make what we have to do difficult. I glance at my brother and recall his ferocious bear. I give myself a mental head shake over my doubts.

CHAPTER 4

Annie

S INCE TRISTAN ARRIVED, I take my morning run later than I prefer. In an effort to avoid his naked glory and my nearly uncontrollable urge to satisfy my lust, I've changed my routine. Carly understands my need and often joins me. But today she's got other plans, and I make my way to the mudroom, where I'll strip down to shift before stepping out into the late-January air.

The floor is cold under my bare feet, and goose bumps form on my arms when I take off my shirt. I notice Tristan's coat and boots set in perfect order. It strikes me as odd, considering his personality oozes chaos. But come to think of it, he does dress impeccably. The vision of his tight butt in jeans that hug his hips flashes in my mind as the familiar stretch of skin and crack of my bones sound as I shift. I shake off the fantasy of Tristan's firm backside in my grip when a cold blast of air greets me as I open the door to step outside.

I flex my powerful thighs and take off in a sprint. My large paws thud in a steady cadence as I move across our lawn and follow the tree line to the meadow. I love being in the woods, but it can be noisy and slow with too much snowfall. We've had a stormy winter, and my feet sink in over two feet of heavy powder. As a bear, the effort to run through is minimal.

I gallop at full bore until my chest aches with the icy air pumping through my taxed lungs, and I slow down to a walk as I catch my breath. I gaze out toward the knoll ahead and smile at the memory of my wedding to Kyle. I envision us as the teenagers we were, giddy with the love true mates have. Sadness washes over me as I get closer, and when I reach the top, I let out a cry. I thump my bottom to the ground to let sorrow escape.

I'm crying for more than my lost mate, though. The pain of not being able to have children is something I'm reminded of every day, living in the same house with my niece and two nephews. Carly and Brady do their best to share them with me, and I had hoped it would ease my longing. But the truth is, I want a family of my own.

Snow has begun to fall, and I lift my snout up to let soft flakes tickle my nose as they melt. Now I've been given a second chance at love with another true mate. This is incredibly lucky, and I should be grateful. But why does Tristan have to be so infuriatingly difficult? Why can't the man who keeps his clothing immaculate figure out that a woman wants to be treasured the same way?

The snow is soft when I fall onto my back and let the chilly earth soothe me. I know I should tell Tristan how I feel, because it's inevitable that we'll end up together. I let out a sigh.

I'm lonely. I had a brief affair with Ian, and while I broke it off because we weren't true mates, it hurt to give up on love. I want to be held and cherished again.

Sitting up, I shake my body to remove the snow, and movement captures my attention. In the distance, a polar bear is running toward me. It's either Isabelle or Tristan. A brief hope flits through me that it's Isabelle. But my senses already know it's not.

Even though Tristan and I are true mates, we can't speak to each other telepathically until we seal our bond with sex and a bite. I decide to show him I can be playful too and jump up to prepare myself to pounce when he gets close enough. I laugh silently as he gets near me, because Carly was right—his fur has a slight orange tint.

He slows and presents me with the perfect opportunity. I release the stored energy of my stance and bowl him over. We roll down the hill in a heap, and I scramble to my feet to run. Tristan takes up the chase, and we bob and weave around each other like football players on a field. Eventually, he tackles me, and I lie under him as I pant in breathlessness.

My heart is beating from more than exertion, and when Tristan lowers his snout to nuzzle in my neck, I cuddle back. When he relaxes, I flip us over to escape and race toward home. This time, Tristan doesn't tease and runs beside me, matching me stride for stride as if we're equals. I stay with him instead of breaking away. I may not be able to use words to convey my message, but I hope my actions show him what it is I need.

When we reach the house, I know I have to shift back in front of him. It's easy to push out of the house as a bear, but it's not quite the same to get inside, and changing into a human usually happens just outside the door. Tristan surprises me by shifting quickly and reaching for the door to hold it open before I have a chance to change. I lumber inside as a bear, and he turns his back to me so I can have privacy.

Once I'm a person again, I say, "Thank you." I'm not sure if I'm rewarding him for his chivalry or if I'm ready to make my move when I add, "You can turn back around."

Heat rises to my cheeks when Tristan moves his blue-eyed scan over my nude body. It's not embarrassment that is heating me up though, and I peruse my true mate with my gaze too. His shoulders are as wide as the doorway, and arms the size of tree trunks frame a torso that is a study in anatomy. The cut muscles of his abdomen lead down to nearly white hair that cushions a cock pulsing as it hardens in desire. *Desire for me.*

When Tristan lets out a shaky breath, I reach out to touch his trembling chest. He grasps my hand and kisses his way up my arm until his teeth graze my shoulder. I shudder, and he says, "You're the most beautiful woman I've ever seen."

His touch sends an electric pulse to my core, and my voice is almost a whisper. My knees get weak. "This is how to get to me."

Tristan's arm snakes around my waist, and he pulls me against his body. "Annie, love. I can't believe you've been able to resist this all because of rules you've set for us."

"Rules? I believe it's common decency."

He chuckles, and the dismissal of my feelings sends a different rush of heat through me as he says, "It won't matter once we mate. I'm an alpha, and you'll be forced to follow whatever I say." He twists one of my curls around his finger and tugs at it.

My anger spikes, and I push at his rock-hard chest to get away. "I should have known this was just an act." I huff and grab my panties from my pile of clothing on the bench. I step in them.

"Don't be that way. You'll want to do as I say, and you know it."

The elastic waistband of my underwear snaps. "I don't think so. I've never taken orders that don't have meaning. Just ask Brady." But the reality is, Tristan might be right. An alpha command is not something you can easily ignore. I've been told you can disobey if you're from an alpha family, but I've never had a reason to test it.

Tristan has my bra in his hands, and he holds it out for me to slip my arms in. It would be a sweet gesture if I weren't so mad. I reach to grab it, and he pulls it out of reach. "Let me do this for you."

I glare at him as I slip my arms into the straps, and he turns me by my shoulders so he can hook it. Tiny hairs stand up on my skin as his touch makes me crave his arms around me again. He drags a finger down my spine and whispers, "You think you need to tame me. But it's the other way around."

I turn to face him and discover he's not smiling. He's serious.

CHAPTER 5

Annie

A METAL BAKING sheet clatters on the stove top as I set it down. The aroma of chocolate chip cookies fills the room. I say, "My vote is to send them to some other clan."

My mother is sitting at the kitchen table, and her spoon clinks against her teacup as she stirs. "Tristan really gets under your skin, doesn't he?"

"That's putting it mildly, Mother." I lift the tray of raw dough and place it in the oven. "Tristan thinks he needs to tame me." I slam the heavy stove door shut. *"Tame me!"*

"You are quite headstrong, dear. Perhaps he didn't mean it in the Neanderthal way."

"You're one to talk. I think you gave me that trait. I recall Dad didn't always have the last say."

"Good point. But when it mattered, we were a unified force." She lifts her teacup to her mouth and blows on the steaming contents. "You'll need to learn to do what's best for his clan."

His clan. If I marry Tristan, I'll be the prima of the De Rozier clan. I shake my head. "Right now, I can't fathom leading anything together peacefully." I also can't fathom the idea of living anywhere but this house. I don't think three alphas in the same residence would work, which means I'll be moving out of my brother's house, which has been my home for the last few years.

"Repeat after me. Marriage is a compromise," says Mom.

I squint my eyes at her. "You're not helping." My spatula scrapes on metal as I slide a cookie off. "Besides, the De Roziers still don't have any land."

"It's in the works. You're going to have to find a way to live with him."

What she's not saying is that I don't have a choice. The draw of true mates is almost impossible to ignore, and I'm stuck with Tristan De Rozier. For life. My bones thud when I fall into the wooden chair across from Mother, and I place a plate stacked with cookies on the table between us. I take a large bite of one and let the sugar race to my bloodstream. Speaking over a mouthful of food, I say, "I feel like the spirits keep punishing me."

Mother reaches out and touches my arm. "It does seem that way at times, doesn't it?"

Ever since I found out I was barren, along with all the women in my clan who are of child-bearing age, it's been one thing after another. Kyle and my father were killed not long after that discovery. And recently we lost one of the women we brought in to save our clan to the same werebears who killed my husband. It would be so easy to hole up in my room and drown myself in my misery.

Fortunately, I'm too strong for that sort of wallowing, and I stand up to get milk. "Help me see the silver lining." White liquid gurgles into my glass.

"You're going to be a prima. You'll have a clan that looks up to you as a leader. You'll no longer be in the shadow of your brother as the Le Roux alpha." I sit back down at the table and she continues. "You have the love and support of your immediate family, and"—she reaches over to place her hand on mine—"Tristan is one hot ticket. I'll bet he's an animal in bed."

I chuckle at my mother's brazen way. I give her some back. "I do think the sex will be hot. Can I survive on that alone?"

Mom winks at me. "It definitely helps smooth over the rough patches."

Great. My destiny is to be with a control freak, but at least I'll have plenty of orgasms. I sigh. "I suppose it could be worse."

"What could be worse?" Carly asks as she enters the kitchen with her baby Audrey.

I reach out to take the small girl. "We're talking about Tristan."

"Annie says she won't mind the sex," says Mother.

Carly chuckles. "No, I bet not. He's smoking hot, and I guess he knows what he's doing."

Donna says, "Fortunately, that's a werebear thing. Never heard of one who couldn't please his mate."

Carly grins. "Don't tell Brady. He thinks he's special."

Mother says, "They all do, and that's how we like it." She stands up to take Audrey from me. "Any word on how Ashton's talk with Tristan went?"

"I got a one-word answer to my question. 'Good,'" says Carly.

I say, "Got to love that man's efficiency."

Mother says, "So let's hope he's got a clue now. Because the scent of unrequited lust in the air is getting old."

I resist the urge to sniff myself. "Mother, sometimes you really shouldn't speak your every thought."

Donna lifts Ashley in the air above her head and gets a squeal. "I thought that was part of my charm."

Carly says, "It is now." She flashes a grin at Mother. "But when we first met, not so much."

I ask, "So tell me about where Brady plans to put the De Roziers. Where is my new home going to be?"

Carly smiles at me in excitement. "Be glad I was at that meeting." She glances around as if Brady's going to pop up from a hidden corner. "Don't tell him I told you, but he's thinking about one thousand acres around the lake where you used to ice skate as kids."

Warmth floods my heart because that's one of my favorite places, and Carly knows it. "Was that your doing?"

She nods as her eyes glisten. "I'm not sure how I'm going to manage here without you, but I want you to be in a special place that will make you happy."

My eyes fill with tears too. I whisper as I pull her into a hug. "Carly."

She squeezes me tight. "You deserve the best."

I pull away and sniff. "Yeah, well, we need to whip that true mate of mine into shape, because right now he's kind of the worst."

Carly frowns. "Yeah, about that. I wouldn't be so sure he's as much of a mess as he wants us to think." She shrugs. "I can't explain it, but Kimi has been teaching me to use my gift, and I sense there's a whole lot more to his story."

Kimi is our medicine woman, and we only recently discovered Carly has untapped magical powers. I think about how orderly Tristan is in his personal habits. The kind of orderly I am, which tells me he's not only got a need for control in our relationship, but I bet he isn't quite the free spirit he tries to portray. "Interesting. Seems I need to get to know Tristan a whole lot better."

Mother perks up. "Does this mean you're going to do him?"

A rush of desire burns in me, and I say, "Yes, Mother. Consider him done."

CHAPTER 6

Isabelle

I STROKE THE smooth fabric of Tristan's comforter while I wait for him to get out of the shower. He left me alone to go work out with Ashton earlier, and I'm bored. I sit on the end of Tristan's bed, and the mattress bounces.

He's rubbing his hair with a towel when he walks into the room, and I say, "I'm thinking about a tattoo."

Tristan stares at me for a moment. "Really? Whatever for?"

"They're beautiful. Have you seen Sierra's?" Sierra is Carly's best friend, and they own a tattoo parlor in town.

"I have, and they are very nice. But why the sudden interest?"

I get up and wander toward his bureau. The usual contents of his pocket are on it and arranged neatly because he placed the phone, small utility knife, and wallet there carefully. The leather case of his phone is smooth in my hand as I pick it up. "I've got nothing else to do."

"You mean drinking too much and riding Mr. So Right Tonight isn't enough?" The fabric of his jeans rustles as he pulls them up.

"Your attempt to shame me isn't working."

"I didn't think it would. But your time would be better spent doing something useful."

I grin at him and lick my lips. "I'm quite useful."

Tristan rolls his eyes at me and buttons up his Oxford shirt. "I mean get a job."

I shudder when I recall the horrible work positions I had to take to help us survive back home. "No."

"You could work at the lumber mill, or the gym, or even the tattoo parlor. All you have to do is ask, and I'm sure the Le Roux would find you something to do."

I don't want a job, so I change the subject. "Speaking of the gym, how was your workout with Ashton? And why wasn't I allowed to come?"

Tristan smiles slowly as he keeps me in suspense. "It was a test to see how well I fight. And some helpful advice on how to win over Annie."

I flip open his phone. Tristan snatches it out of my hand as I ask, "And how did it go?"

"I impressed Ash with my skills and pretended to listen to his speech about honor and trust." He glances over at his bed. "It might be time to make my move."

I snort. "You act so in control, but I know how true mates work. You want her as badly as she wants you. Why don't you be your charming self and get laid tonight?"

Tristan rolls up the sleeves of his crisp white shirt to reveal his strong forearms. "Not a bad idea, Izzy. Not a bad idea at all."

I follow my brother as he makes his way downstairs. Annie seems to bake every day, and my mouth waters at the aroma of something chocolate that awaits us in the kitchen. When we enter, Annie is at the table with her mother.

Donna says, "My two favorite polar bears. Come. Have some milk and cookies with us."

Tristan sits next to Donna and pours on the charm as I pour us two drinks. He says, "I can never refuse my two favorite black bear. You look lovely today, Donna."

She replies, "And you as well, Tristan. How was your session with Ashton?"

"Grueling. He's a tough warrior."

I hand my brother a glass of milk and sit down across from him. The scent of Annie's arousal is pungent, and I smile as I speak in my brother's head. *"She's practically sliding off her chair."*

Tristan turns his attention to Annie. He licks his lips slowly and says, "Delicious."

She masks her desire well. "You haven't even taken a bite."

My brother lowers his voice to a sexy growl. "I can tell by the smell."

I let out a disgusted noise from the back of my throat, and he flashes me a smile before he says, "I enjoyed running with you this morning. Any chance we can slip out for a movie or coffee later tonight?"

"Tristan De Rozier, are you asking me out? On a date?"

He puts a finger in his mouth and slowly removes it as if he's licking off chocolate. It lingers on his lower lip. Annie sucks in a breath before he replies, "I sure am."

Donna chuckles, and Annie says, "I'd like that." Her hand moves up to her neckline, and she tugs on it as if she can't breathe. Tristan's gaze follows as her movement reveals her cleavage. He mutters in my mind. *"Holy mother of God, I could take her right on the table."*

I ask, "Should Donna and I leave you two alone?"

Annie shakes her head and stands abruptly. "No, of course not." She walks quickly to the fridge and asks, "More milk, anyone?"

I decide to give Annie time to recover. "Donna, do you think Carly would be interested in some help at Ink It?"

"I bet she would. Are you running out of *activities* to keep you entertained?"

Donna is blunt about sex, and the only time I've seen her contain her thoughts is around Annie. Because I appreciate her candor, I answer, "Amazingly, I need more to feel fulfilled. Who knew?"

Donna grins at me as Annie returns to her seat. She says, "Yes. I imagine you do. Balance, after all."

Tristan has leaned back and has his arms crossed over his chest. "Balance is good." He glances at Annie's chest and then back up to her face. "Anticipation is even better.

Don't you think, Annie?" He raises his eyebrows at her.

She leans forward on her arms and squeezes her breasts with them to offer my brother an eyeful. "Sometimes the reward is worth waiting for."

Donna's eyes widen, and it reinforces the fact that Annie doesn't flirt like this easily. *"Holy crap, brother. She's penciled you in. I'll pass out the earplugs for later."*

His laughter comes through before he says, *"You do that. Because I'm going to make sure the whole house knows she's mine."*

A twinge of jealousy grips my heart, because I haven't met the man who makes me want to scream his name yet, and I'm afraid I never will.

Tristan's eyebrows rise just the slightest as he glances at me. *"Tonight would be a good time for your date as well."*

I give him the slightest nod, because our plan is working beautifully. *"Indeed it is."*

CHAPTER 7

Annie

O NCE I DECIDE to do something, I can be like a torpedo racing toward my target and blasting through anything in my way. My decision to mate with Tristan is solid, and after I put a lasagna in the oven, I come to my room to prepare for my evening. Steam fills the bathroom as water splashes in the tub. My skin is already overheated with lust, and the ache between my legs is begging for relief. I'm tempted to do something about that and open a cabinet before I can stop myself. *Anticipation.*

The wooden door slams shut as I push it with a bit more force than necessary. It's been a while since I've had a man satisfy my needs, and I'd rather wait for the real thing. I shudder and close my eyes while the fantasy of what Tristan's body against me, on me, and in me would feel like plays in my mind. I sigh and step into the lavender-scented water of my bath. Heat envelops me as I sink in.

I lean back against the edge and stretch out my limbs.

I gaze down at my shapely legs, and the hair I notice makes me sit up to grab a razor. Excitement courses through me as I think about my date. Dare I hope Tristan will be charming the whole time instead of displaying his annoying side?

Water trickles as I raise my leg to scrape over it and remove stubble. Tonight is going to mark the beginning of a new Chapter in my life. I'd gotten quite comfortable being Brady's sidekick, the alpha's sister. And when Carly came along, I settled into taking care of them, along with the children who were born a few months ago. While they hired a nanny to help with the triplets, and we have a cleaning lady, Brady and Carly are going to have to start cooking for themselves when I leave. I should look into a chef for them.

I snort at myself. Carly is more than capable of figuring out what to do for meals, and I ought to be planning for my new home instead of worrying about my brother's family. The triplets' squirming bodies and sweet faces flash in my mind, and my heart gets heavy as I realize I won't be seeing them as much as I do now. While I look forward to setting up my new home as the prima of the De Rozier clan, I can't help but wish that included children of my own.

Plastic clatters as I set my razor down on the edge of the tub. I'm being foolish, longing for something I'll never have. I need to be happy with what I've been given, because it's amazing, considering I'd resigned myself to life as a widow and doting aunt. I grab a washcloth and finish my bath.

As I'm toweling off, a knock sounds on my bedroom door. Carly speaks to me in my head. *"It's me."*

"Come on in."

Soft carpet cushions my feet as I make my way to my dresser, and my sister-in-law enters. My bed whooshes as she sits herself on the end of it. She asks, "Are you excited for tonight?"

My drawer thuds open, and silky fabric is smooth in my hands as I search for a bra and panty set for Tristan's eyes. "Yes, because it's about time. But no, because I'm afraid he'll let the jerk side show."

"My suggestion is to try to control your anger and be honest. Tell him how it makes you feel and be rational. I bet he'll respond better to logic."

I bend down to place my breasts in the cups of my bra before I stand and hook it. "I'll try." I glance at Carly and add, "But being rational with that man is hard to do."

Carly smiles at me, but it fades quickly into a frown. She says, "There's something I need to tell you. I only remembered it today, and it's important you know."

"Okay."

"Isabelle mentioned this in passing, and I had forgotten until tonight. Tristan has children."

"What?" My stomach clenches. Has my true mate been mated before? Who is she? Where is she? And more importantly, where are the children? I walk over and sink down on the bed next to Carly as she twists to face me.

She says, "I don't know much more than that. It was

Christmas Day, and Isabelle mentioned that she thought you were a good match for Tristan. She said it wouldn't be a problem because the next alpha of the De Roziers was already secured and something about the mother being gone."

"Great. That'll be a handy conversation starter." It figures there would have to be one more thing to make mating with Tristan difficult.

"I know, right? I'm sorry I didn't tell you this sooner. I'm not sure why I'd forgotten it."

I reach out and take Carly's hand. "Maybe because we had a rather big crisis at that time where we lost Taylor." When Victor Veilleux kidnapped Sierra's babies, a group of us went to rescue them. The fight that occurred killed our enemy as well as our fiercest female warrior. She was one of the women we called here to be turned into a werebear and provide children. "I know you felt incredible guilt for bringing her here, and I bet that took precedence in your mind."

Carly squeezes my fingers. "I still do. But I have to learn to live with it." She releases her grip. "Anyway. I'm glad I remembered in time so you enter your relationship with Tristan knowing what you're getting into."

I nod and stand up to walk over to my closet. This news changes things, and my need to mate is not as paramount as it was a few minutes ago. No. Now information is what I crave. I grab my favorite knit dress without thinking and tug it off the hanger. Mating with Tristan will lead to becoming more than a prima. I'll be a stepmother too. Soft wool caresses my skin as I slip the garment over my head and pull it down. I recall how moments ago I was longing for a family of my own that involved more than a husband. I squat down to find my matching shoes. *Careful what you wish for, Annie. You just might get it.*

CHAPTER 8

Isabelle

THE LE ROUX think I'm out for another night on the town. I've played my part well, and now that they're convinced my goal in life is to destroy my liver and reputation, slipping off to meet our contact face to face is going to be a breeze.

Annie's busy with Tristan tonight, and their inevitable mating is the perfect disguise for my excitement. I try to contain it as I make my way to the kitchen and another delicious dinner prepared by my future sister-in-law. She's going to be a great asset to the De Roziers in more ways than one.

I enter into the chaos of triplet-feeding time. Three high chairs are set up, and Annie, Carly, and the nanny are spooning vivid-colored goo into tiny mouths. Although it seems to cover their faces better. Squeals sound, and I grin at the adorable children. I ask, "Annie, do you need me to check on dinner?"

"Yes, please. Can you pull the tinfoil off the lasagna to let the top brown?"

"Sure." I open the oven and let the hot steam escape before bending down to tug at the aluminum cover. Bits of cheese stick to it, and I pull them off to sample the pasta. Salty flavor coats my tongue as the stove door thumps shut.

Dinner for the babies is followed by bath time, and I often finish preparations for our meal to let Annie help. I say, "I'll make the salad and garlic bread while you all go for a swim."

Annie stands up first to pull a child from the high chair. I don't know why it surprises me that she's in a nice dress with only the sleeves rolled up and still remains spot free. That woman seems to be good at everything she does. Even the kid she fed is the cleanest of the bunch. She says, "I won't be taking a second bath tonight. I'll let little Everett's mother do that."

Carly chuckles as she leads the way out of the kitchen. I think about the brats who are Tristan's children. He's got five-year-old triplets who are holy terrors. Their mother didn't take to child-rearing, and my brother was too busy trying to save a clan to deal with them himself. Now they reside with my mother, who farms them out to a revolving door of nannies. Annie's going to have her work cut out for her when they come to live here.

A tray clicks as I remove it from a high chair, and I deposit it in the sink. Water rushes when I flip it on. My thoughts make me wonder if Annie knows about Tristan's kids. If it weren't important that the two mate soon, I'd be happy to toss out that little grenade at the table tonight, but I'll resist because I'd be hurting myself too by trying to sabotage their relationship just for the satisfaction of watching my brother squirm.

I'm still cleaning when Annie returns. She says, "Thank you, Isabelle. It's been really nice having your help these past few weeks."

"You're welcome. It's the least I can do. Tristan and I really appreciate your hospitality."

Wheels rumble over the tile floor as Annie moves the high chairs against the wall where they currently live. "I'm probably speaking too soon, but since we know I'm eventually going to be a De Rozier, I hope you realize I'd like for you to live with us." She turns to me as I open the fridge to get the vegetables for the salad. "I have a thing about family being close."

"I've noticed. And if you plan to keep me well fed like now, I'd be happy to live with you." I throw in a bit to go with my cover story and my alibi tonight. "But I wonder if you're thinking clearly. I fear you don't approve of my wild side."

A large bowl clatters on the counter, and Annie says, "Oh, no. I'm sorry if I gave you that impression. I'm quite aware of our animal urges. I'm more concerned about what drives you to be so reckless."

She hands me a cutting board, and the wood handle is cool in my palm. I turn from her gaze abruptly so she doesn't discover my shock. I can't recall a time that someone really cared enough about my well-being to be worried about me. "No reason. I'm a free spirit and want to taste adventure before I settle down."

My knife chops steadily as I slice a cucumber. I stop and resist the urge to glance over at Annie. "I'm merely sowing my wild oats, as my grandmother would say."

Annie smiles at me. "Glad to hear it. Because I care about you."

My ice cube of a heart might be glistening as it melts a little at her kindness. "I care about you too. I'm glad you're Tristan's true mate. He deserves a good woman like you."

She snorts. "I'm not sure about that. I think I'm about to test him as much as he tests me."

Without thinking, I reply, "That's a good thing. Tristan needs someone to call him on things and remind him that being the alpha doesn't always mean he's right." I wince internally at my words. I'm supposed to be playing him off as carefree and make her think he'll be easy to manage.

Annie just nods, and it occurs to me she already knows about his need for control. She confirms it when she says, "I suspect our first fights are going to be epic as we battle for power over running the household." She flicks the bread knife at me in jest. "I hope he's prepared to die before I compromise over anything in the kitchen, because this is my domain."

I grin at her. "As long as you promise to keep cooking, I've got your back." Surprisingly, I think I do. I like Annie and want to be her friend. But dread wraps around my insides with a firm grip as I think about the next phase of the plan I'm about to set in motion tonight. Eventually, friendship with Annie will be out of the question.

Heat blows Annie's curls as she puts the bread in the oven. She's welcomed us with open arms since day one. It's unfortunate she won't trust so easily when we're through.

I catch myself before I sigh. I'm getting too involved if I'm beginning to care about what happens to Annie. I focus on the prize, and my encounter later tonight. One thing the De Roziers do well is win. And nothing's going to stand in the way of Tristan and me getting what we want.

CHAPTER 9

Annie

T HE MOMENT TRISTAN'S foot finds mine under the dinner table, I know we need to finish things up quickly, before I lose myself in the intensity of our attraction. I still need to clear up the issue of his children he neglected to share. Although once we mate, I might be able to think more clearly.

My chair scrapes on the tile as I push away from the table to begin to clear dishes. Carly says, "Just one trip. You have a date."

I set my plate on the counter and turn to her. "Thank you." I glance at Tristan and try not to focus on the plump lips I'd like to sample for dessert. "I'm going to go upstairs and get my things."

"Me too," he says and gets up to follow me.

A low growl comes from him once we begin to climb the steps, and my insides twinge in reaction to the sound and the knowledge that he's looking at my bottom and likes what he sees. I'm not a thin woman, like most werebear, and I know my round backside tempts many a male's hands. But right now, there's only one I want touching it, and it would be so easy to yank him into my bedroom and skip the pretenses.

I shake off my lust and focus on the conversation we need to have before I give him my physical commitment. I pause by my door to turn and speak to Tristan. "I'll meet you in the Hummer."

Tristan shakes his head. "This is a date. Wait by your door if I'm not back before you're ready. I'm walking you to the car, and I plan to drive."

I smile and give him a tiny nod before entering my room. He does know how to court me. I walk over to the bathroom to brush my teeth and check my makeup. Lipstick slides slowly over my lips as they burn in anticipation of being kissed. I take my time so Tristan will be waiting when I'm done.

When I'm ready, I sense he's outside my door, and I pause to inhale his scent before I open it. I savor the electricity that races through me. Soon I'll associate his smell with an intense reality, but for now the fantasy of what's to come is a darn good motivator to remove the barrier between us. I exit my room.

Tristan offers me his arm, and we descend the stairs side by side, as if we've been doing it for years. "You fit next to me well. Just like when we were running together as bear."

I gaze up at his icy-blue eyes. They're like the pools of crystal-clear water I imagine exist in his homeland. "It's a true mate thing. But I fear we're going to have more struggles than most."

Tristan grins at me, and his teeth sparkle in the entryway light as he pulls on the heavy front door. "Nothing we won't be able to handle, love."

I step through, and the contents of my purse rustle as I reach in and find the compartment that contains my car keys. I hand them to him. "Good. Now here's my first compromise. I'll let you drive my car."

Tristan takes the keys with one hand and holds my fingers with his other as he brings it up to his lips. He kisses the back of my hand and whispers, "To many more."

I smile as he leads me to the passenger's side and lets me in. The engine roars softly when he turns it over and says, "I think we should go get dessert. I'm afraid I won't be able to concentrate on a movie with you next to me in the dark. I may not be appropriate."

I know what you mean. "Good idea. A table between us might help me keep my focus. I have something I need to ask you."

"No need to wait. I'll tell you anything. Ask me now."

"Okay." I take a deep breath. "Tell me about your children."

Tristan cuts me a quick glance, and I notice he doesn't appear surprised. "I wondered when that would come up."

"I only just found out. Why didn't you mention it sooner?"

"I thought you knew." The Hummer bumps over the

snow-covered dirt road toward town.

"Why would you think that?" I ask.

"Because I expect your family researched mine the way we did yours. I doubt I have many secrets."

"You haven't been easy to research. You've lived a pretty secretive life by nature of your location."

The car slows, and Tristan pulls over to a section of the road that has a wide shoulder designed for heavy equipment to get out of the way of traffic or for turning around. "Let me give you my full attention."

His action surprises me. "Thank you."

He takes my hands and rubs over the backs with his thumbs. "While you've had a true mate you lost, I never found one and married for the sole purpose of carrying on my family name. As you can imagine, it didn't work out so well."

I think I see sorrow in his face and say, "I'm sorry. Was your breakup painful?"

"It was messy. Magda left the clan."

"Did she take your children?" I notice how warm his hands are as he continues to hold mine. They're almost hot.

"No. My mother cares for them."

"You must miss them."

He shrugs. "They're better off without me. I don't have time to devote to raising children."

The man has been with us for more than two weeks doing as he pleases as if this is a vacation, and he doesn't have time for his kids? I pull my hands away. "Children need their father, even if it's only for brief periods of time."

"You haven't got any idea what my kingdom is like, Annie. Our kind is dwindling in numbers, and those who are left are working like dogs to survive. I don't have time to play games."

My mother bear instincts kick in, and I react to his dismissal of his children's needs. "But you've had no trouble treating your time here like a holiday." As soon as the words come out of my mouth, I wish I could take them back. I've always had a roof over my head and food in my belly. I've had more than most, and I cringe that I reacted so callously.

He glares at me. "That's what you think we've been doing? Your clan just killed an enemy, and the Veilleux eliminated one of your best warriors. Isabelle and I have been patiently waiting to make our arrangement and trying to be sensitive to your loss." He thumps a hand down on the steering wheel, and it shudders under the impact. "But hey, let's call your brother and get the deal done. Because we wouldn't want me to be frolicking in the snow while I should be reading bedtime stories to my children."

Tristan grabs my face in his hands. "And we might as well get the true mate bond over with too." His kiss is rough, and I try to pull back. His tongue plunges into my mouth, and while my body is responding with urgency, my mind is furious at his attack. I pound on his chest, and he loosens his hold.

I break away. "Stop."

His release is abrupt, and I realize he had no intention of taking things further. He asks, "What's the matter? Don't you want efficiency?"

Hot shame burns my cheeks, and I'm grateful for the near darkness surrounding us. But I know it's not hiding anything, because moonlight illuminates Tristan's face, and the muscles in his jaw are flexed as I say, "I'm sorry. You're right. I don't know what it's been like for you. That was a careless thing for me to say."

Tristan turns the key and shifts the car into drive. He pulls out without speaking, and we drive to town in silence. As tempted as I am to speak, I refrain and let his anger dissipate. I gaze out at the widening funnel of light that bounces off the snowbanks and dark shadows of pine trees that line the side of the street. My lips are swollen and burn under my tongue when I lick them. Eventually the car tires crunch over the frozen bits of snow in the parking lot of the Sweetery, a local bakery and coffee shop that caters to the college kids in town.

Tristan pulls into a spot, and when he turns off the car, he says, "I'll answer any questions you have. But I'm beginning to doubt the wisdom of our union."

I want to crawl in a hole with the guilt I feel. I'm embarrassed at my elitist attitude, and any appetite I had for dessert is gone. "I'm so sorry, Tristan. I've ruined our date. Why don't we go home?"

He sighs, "That's a good idea."

We ride home in silence, and I mentally kick myself

as I replay the mean things I said in an endless loop. I recall Carly saying the spirits are supposed to give us what we need. Did they think I needed to be knocked off my high horse? Consider me on the ground, wiping off the dirt, because I feel about as worthy as a pile of manure right now.

I sigh too and hope tomorrow I can make up for my selfish ways.

CHAPTER 10

Isabelle

I GLANCE IN the rearview mirror of the truck I borrowed from the Le Roux, and I brush off a flake of mascara from under my eye. I applied dark liner for a smoky look that spelled out seduction. In case that's not enough, I'm wearing a halter top in shimmery gold that is merely a patch of fabric covering my breasts and stomach. It could easily blow up and offer a magnificent view of all I have to offer. The tight leather skirt I wore leaves little else to the imagination. I'm dressed for sex.

I pluck my way carefully across the icy parking lot. My stiletto heels aren't easy to walk in, but the effect of the added height makes me even more noticeable. I wonder if the man I'm meeting will be able to compete.

When I enter the Jefferson Manor, a historical building turned into a restaurant, I command the attention of almost everyone. I saunter toward the hostess station. "I have a reservation for De Rozier."

A pretty girl glances up at me and says, "Yes, your date is already here. Right this way." She leads me through a room full of tables, and I smile as I catch the eye of more than one male admirer. No need to be cold when any one of them could become my next conquest. Although tonight is reserved for the man I'm meeting for dinner.

The moment the dark-blond guy stands up, my bear begins to growl in appreciation. He's delicious, with his broad shoulders and bit of hair coming out of the top of his dress shirt. His lips are ruby red and beg to be bitten as he comes toward me. "Isabelle."

He takes my hand, and it's clear he possesses the alpha family effect on women by the way my skin tingles in invitation for those fingers to touch more. "Luke."

"You're more stunning than I was told." He lifts my hand to kiss it, and the sensation of his damp lips on my skin races right to my core. My mind imagines how they'd feel in more intimate places, and every werebear in the room has to know what I'm thinking by my scent.

I'm not alone in my attraction, because Luke's eyes are heavy, and he doesn't release me when I say, "And you're more charming. It's a pleasure to meet you."

"Come. Sit." He places a hand on the bare skin of my lower back and guides me to a chair. *He can't stop touching me.* And I don't want him to.

He places me in a chair next to him instead of across the table, and when Luke lowers himself to his seat, his thigh brushes along mine. I notice a decanter of red wine on the table of white linen. The candle flickers as if it's having trouble breathing too.

Luke says, "I hope you don't mind, but I took the liberty of ordering us a wine. It should be open now and ready to drink."

I have no idea what he means by open. I'm a straight whisky girl. But I don't give my ignorance away. I watch as the liquid gurgles into a wide globe-like glass, and he hands it to me. "Give it a try and let me know what you think."

I sniff it like I've seen in the movies and then take a sip. The flavor reminds me a bit of something bitter but is followed by something slightly fruity. It's not bad, and I decide I could get used to it. "Lovely." I take another swallow as if I'm confirming it.

Luke's glass is now full too, and he lifts it up for a toast. "To a long and profitable relationship."

Glass clinks as we join our goblets, and we take another drink. The flavor has quickly grown on me. I say, "This wine is addicting." I take another sip because I meant it. I can't seem to stop.

Warmth on my thigh surprises me as Luke's hand lands just above my knee. He strokes my skin with a finger and speaks in a low voice. "Intoxicating, isn't it?"

He doesn't waste any time. I'm used to being the one who makes inappropriate advances. But they usually happen in a bar and not a formal restaurant. I surprise myself when I spread my legs a little as an invitation, and he moves his hand a little further up my leg. I breathe out. "Yes." But my mind begs me to focus, because I have a purpose for this meeting.

I clear my throat. "Things are moving along smoothly."

Luke continues to stroke my skin, and his fingers move the tiniest bit higher with each one. "Tristan is in place?"

"Yes." I slide forward on the chair, and the movement hikes my skirt up as I perch on the edge. I widen my thighs a little more. "He's positioned himself nicely."

"Good. And nobody suspects anything?"

Holy hell. If he keeps this up, I'm going to come in a dining room full of people. I lift my glass and glance around the room. Conversations are low, and nobody is paying us any attention. "No. Nobody has any idea what we're up to."

My hips thrust of their own accord in a barely perceptible movement that mimics the flexing of my core. Luke leans in closer to me, and his breath is warm on my cheek. I take in air sharply as his finger strokes under my panties and in my folds. He whispers, "Let's keep it that way."

I take a sip of my wine and swallow with a gulp when he slides two digits inside me. I have one hand under the table too, and I grip the edge of my chair to dig my nails into the wood. My eyelids are heavy, and I let them fall for a second as I moan softly. I set the glass of wine down and say, "That's heavenly."

"I'm glad you like it." Luke's fingers are curled, and he's moving them quickly as his thumb presses against my clit. My belly is trembling as waves of pleasure wash over me, signaling my approaching orgasm. A low growl comes from Luke as he says, "My attraction to you is quite a surprise."

I croak out, "You don't do this with all the girls?"

He chuckles and then says, "No. This is a first."

It is for me too, and I grab the menu to hide my flushed face. My head swims, and I struggle to keep from crying out.

He whispers, "This is just the appetizer. Wait until you experience the meal."

I shudder with my silent screams as I bite my lip and drop my head to hide my ecstasy. I whisper, "Oh, God." The menu falls to the table with a soft thud.

When I cease trembling, Luke trails his wet fingers down my leg slowly as he retreats. The waitress has arrived and asks if we're ready to order. She's looking at me, and I come back down to earth to say, "I'm sorry. I need a minute."

Luke says, "She'll have the salmon, and I'll take the duck."

When the server leaves, I ask, "Are you always this commanding?"

"Yes." Luke smirks. "My apologies. We hardly know each other." He leans back in his chair and spreads his legs in a casual pose. "Did I not give you what you wanted?"

If we weren't in public, I'd tear open his slacks and take more. Luke's forward way is a huge turn on, and I've forgotten the purpose of our meeting. All I can think about is getting him out of here and someplace where I have no restraints. I glance at his crotch and say, "The night is young. I trust I'll have the opportunity to take what I need."

Luke reaches forward for his wine. He swirls the burgundy liquid around and holds it up to the light. The color reminds me of fresh blood as he says, "We're going to make a good team."

I glance at his throat, and an overwhelming desire to bite him floods my thoughts. I blink quickly to clear my head. *What's wrong with me?* One orgasm, and I want him to be my mate? I take another sip of wine and wish I had something harder instead. "Yes. I believe we will."

CHAPTER 11

Isabelle

I RAP LIGHTLY on Tristan's door. It's early, and since I didn't hear any grunting or screams, I know Annie's not in his bed. He opens the door, and I gaze at my brother's hair standing on end as he rubs a hand over his stubbly chin. "C'mon in."

I wander over to his bureau and move the pocket-knife so it's crooked as I ask, "How was your date?"

Tristan sits on his bed and leans against the head-board with his arms crossed over his chest. "It didn't go as planned. I had hoped to get sex before the guilt trip." He lifts his palms up as he shrugs. "But mission accomplished."

"Tell me about it."

Tristan breaks into a grin and leans forward with the excitement of a small boy. "It was beautiful, Izzy. I couldn't have planned it any better. Annie got all over me about the kid thing and accused me of being lazy." His eyes sparkle as he continues. "Once she learned about our past, she was so ashamed. She's going to come begging for me now." He leans back against his headboard again, and it thumps against the wall. My mind flashes to last night with Luke, and I push the memory away. But my stomach remains unsettled. He puts his arms behind his head and says, "And I'm going to love every minute."

I pick up his pocketknife. "Of course you are. But for more than the fact that you won." I roll the smooth plastic coating of the knife around in my hand. I recall the silky-soft skin of Luke's cock, and my fingers long to stroke it. I huff at my silly thought. I don't need Luke to satisfy me when I have a town full of eligible men. "I'm a little worried about the true mate bond you'll have. You realize you won't be able to keep from caring. That's going to make things hard."

"Ah, dear Izzy, you underestimate me. Have you for-gotten I don't have a heart? One can't be ruled by love if the capability doesn't exist."

I shake my head at my brother's brave words as I sit on the edge of his bed. I wonder if he actually believes them. My father was a weak but evil man who loved the bottle more than people. Coupled with the cruel hand of my mother, Tristan and I learned to trust only each other. Fear dances through my veins.

He's all I've got, and if I lose him to Annie, I'll be all alone. My voice is child-like when I ask, "Don't you love me?"

Tristan pulls me into a hug, and I lay my head on his chest. "Of course I do." He strokes my hair and reminds me of when we were little. "You're always mine to protect, Izzy. Never doubt that." He releases me and asks, "So tell me about your night. Did you plant the seed of desire in our dear boy?"

I nod with a big grin as I pull away from him. Luke and I barely got through dinner, and the moment we were done, I went to his car and gave him dessert in the parking lot before I extracted myself to drive to his house for more. "He wants to lick me like an ice cream cone. He's cute, so I might let him." I tilt my head at my brother. "Oh wait"—I chuckle—"I did."

Tristan lets out a low growl. "I don't like that you're having all the fun. I hope Annie plans to grovel soon. I need some relief."

"She's in the kitchen. Should I ask her to bring you up a tray?"

Tristan waggles his eyebrows. "Breakfast in bed? Perhaps you should."

"Done." I push off the bed and pad toward the bureau to return Tristan's knife. "She made blueberry muffins."

Tristan growls again. "It's not muffins I'm hungry for."

I laugh as I move toward the door. On my way down the stairs, I replay my encounter with Luke once again. He was quite an attentive lover, and I can't seem to get him out of my mind. Tristan's right. He got the short straw.

CHAPTER 12

Annie

T RISTAN HASN'T COME down for breakfast yet, and I wonder if he's still mad at me for the things I said last night. I wander to the window and gaze out at the white carpet of snow. I imagine what it must be like to have the home you've always known slowly disappear right under your feet.

My supersensitive hearing detects the creak of the stairs, and I turn to Isabelle entering the kitchen. She says, "Your blueberry muffins smell so good they woke me up."

I wave my arm toward the counter. "Help yourself." She stares at me with a frown, and I ask, "What?"

"I heard your date didn't go so well last night."

I let out a sigh. "Yeah. It's been a long time since I've hurt someone unintentionally like that. I hope Tristan can find a way to forgive me."

Isabelle lifts her eyebrows with a smile. "He loves your muffins. Maybe a little room service would help."

"He's not mad at me?"

She shakes her head. "No. Tristan doesn't hold grudges. But he's a man, and a little sucking up goes a long way."

I turn to her, and the smirk on her face makes me flush when I get her meaning. "Right." I pull a plate from the counter, and a muffin is warm in my hand when I grab it. I place three on a plate and grab a knife to cut off a chunk of butter to go with them.

Isabelle is busy with coffee, and she hands me a mug. "Just the way he likes it."

"Thanks. Wish me luck."

She grins at me. "You don't need it. Now go make my brother happy."

Halfway up the stairs, the aroma of coffee is replaced with the scent of my true mate, and any fear I had is drowned out with desire. By the time I knock on his door, he's probably smelled what's on my mind.

I enter his room when he answers me to find him sitting up in his bed. The covers are low on his waist, and my eyes are drawn to the teasing placement of the sheet. I snap them up to his face. A day-old beard makes him sexier than ever, and the odor of his musk practically makes me swoon. I croak out, "I come with a peace offering."

Tristan pats the bed next to him. "Join me?"

I open my mouth like a gaping fish and try to find words to keep the inevitable from happening. I want in that bed, and he knows it. My footsteps are barely audible as I walk slowly over to him. I remove my slippers and place a knee on the edge. He whips the covers off to let me in. "I won't bite." His grin gets wider, and he adds, "Actually, maybe I will."

Tristan takes the mug I hand him, and I slide over to be next to him. Placing the plate on my lap, I occupy myself with buttering a muffin. When I finish, I offer him a piece. "Here."

He opens his mouth for me to feed him, so I break off a piece and place it on his tongue. I watch him chew it slowly. When we get to the last bite, he grabs my wrist and sucks on one of my fingers. I pull it out slowly and try not to ooze onto the bed in a quaking heap of need. He says, "I can't decide what tastes better. You or the butter."

This time I avoid the trout mouth and don't try to reply. Tristan's coffee mug thumps on the side table, and he moves the plate to join it. When he's done, he stares into my eyes. "You're forgiven. Now let's move on, shall we?"

I nod as he lifts my chin with a finger. He leans in and kisses me. This time he's gentle, and his tongue tests me, waiting for entry. I part my lips and let passion take over. Tristan pulls me close against his chest, and I thread my fingers through his thick hair. The taste of baked goods makes way to his unique flavor, and I drink it in. Our mouths progress into something hungry.

Somehow I find myself on my back, and he's moved on top of me. The pajamas I have on are in the way, and I break away panting to say, "Too many clothes."

Tristan growls and grabs my shirt with both hands to rip it open. The tearing of fabric sends a bolt of desire through me, and I growl back as I arch up to his mouth as it descends onto my breast. He suckles me and draws my nipple between his teeth to give it a tweak. I moan in response.

His breath tickles against my moist skin, and he breathes out, "Annie." I squirm under him as he nips his way down my belly and reaches my pants. He spares them from my shirt's fate and tugs them over my hips. "The scent of you drives me wild."

"Uh-huh." His breath is hot on the junction between my legs, and I'm having trouble with coherent thought. A cry escapes when he swipes his tongue over my clit. "You," he says.

"What?"

"You taste better."

My voice is barely audible when I say, "Oh." He returns to his mission. "Oh!" Cotton is wadded in my palms as I clench the sheets and hang on and climb higher with my exhilaration. Tristan is relentless, and even after I scream, he continues with his hand, bringing me to the brink again within a minute of my previous orgasm.

This time when I'm calling out his name, he rises over me to straddle my chest. I grab his large cock and stroke it as I recover. He says, "I want to be in your mouth."

I move to let him lay down on his back, and when I begin to crawl down to his groin, Tristan grabs my arms.

"Turn around so I can pleasure you at the same time."

I straddle his face and lean down to swipe my tongue over the tip of his dick. He groans and says, "Suck me hard."

His grip on my hips is firm as he tastes me again. I moan around his cock as I suck him in and slide him out in a rhythmic motion. Tristan's hips buck up and move erratically as he gets close, and I take more of him as I approach my own release. He's using both his hand and his mouth, and I'm struggling to give Tristan my best as I pump my hips too.

I cry out with my climax, and the sound is muffled by the thick length filling my mouth. I suck harder and faster to bring Tristan the same pleasure. Heat explodes in my throat, and I gulp down his salty essence as he screams out my name. I savor every drop of his nectar until he's completely flaccid.

I climb up to lay my head on his sweat-slicked chest, and his voice rumbles under my ear. "That's my idea of breakfast."

I grin and rise up to look down at him. "I hope you don't think you're done."

His eyes widen a bit before he chuckles. He says, "You're a bit of a vixen, swallowing me down like that. I didn't expect it."

"No? I guess I do appear reserved, don't I?"

Tristan rolls me over so he's hovering over me. "I approve. What else do you like? Maybe a little dirty talk?"

I grin at him as I reach down to hold his cock. "Try

me."

Tristan growls and nips at my neck as he whispers the naughty things he has planned. And then we do them all.

An hour later, I rub my sleepy eyes and sit up to say, "I need a shower and have to go in to work soon."

"And I'm supposed to work out with Ian. But I'm not sure I have the strength." Tristan pulls a lock of my hair and tugs hard enough that I lean down when he wants me. He speaks softly. "I'll be thinking about you while you're gone, and I want you to think about me."

He shoves a finger inside my sore channel and pumps it in and out, slicking the juices of us over my clit. I shudder in response, and he says, "Think of the things I do to you and imagine more. I plan to give you your every fantasy, and you'll give me mine."

I freeze and envision another woman joining us. Tristan takes his wet finger and places it on my lips. "Don't be afraid." He sticks it in my mouth, and I taste us as I suck lightly. "You'll want to do what I ask."

His finger leaves my mouth with a pop, and he lowers his mouth to kiss me. I relax because if it feels as good as what we just did, then I will want his fantasies. I lose myself in the magic of true mate attraction.

CHAPTER 13

Tori

THE BLARING OF my phone alarm breaks through my sleepy fog, and I groan before I tap the screen to stop the noise. "No."

The sarcastic voice of my roommate, Lucy, calls out. "Rise and shine."

I burrow deeper into my covers and grasp at the lingering memory of my dream. A super-hot guy with dark hair and blue eyes was the star of my sexual fantasy. The one who's been in my dreams for almost two years now. Sometimes he fades away for a while, like this past month. I smile because I'm happy to have my dream guy back. It's the reason I decided to come to the University of Maine at Orono, even though my two triplet sisters picked Bowdoin.

Lucy says, "Tori!" She whips the covers off my body, and the cold air whisks my happy thoughts away. "You may be able to skip calculus, but I can't. If I fail another class, I'm being cut off."

"Fine. Make me coffee." I climb out of the bed and

shuffle over to my closet to retrieve my shower things. Lucy's parents put their foot down about her latest grades, and she's desperate, knowing her party days are numbered. Apparently she'd be forced to cut trees or something if she doesn't get her act together. I've promised to tutor her through this class, but that girl doesn't have the head for math. It's going to be a long semester.

As my flip-flops slap against the tile hallway, my hip itches, and I scratch over the bone where my paw-print tattoo is. I got it before break, and when I get into the bathroom, I inspect it to make sure nothing's wrong. *Huh.* It's not red, but for a second it looks like it is pulsing.

Maybe it's calling me. I shake my head as I remember the woman who gave me my tattoo. The metal hooks holding a vinyl shower curtain rasp over the bar when I yank it open to flip on the water. She said the guy in my dreams was real and it was some freaky cosmic match-making thing. I still wonder what kind of drugs she was on when that theory came to her. As soon as I got inked, I was so out of there.

I step under the hot spray, and the aroma of dirt like from a garden makes me open my eyes to make sure I'm in the dorm bathroom. *Whoa.* I cup water in my hands and discover it's normal. How strange. I shrug it off when I realize someone probably watered their half-dead plants in the shower.

When I return to my room, I notice a steaming cup of black coffee on my dresser. I grab it and gulp down a burning mouthful. While my dreams are welcome back in my life, the lack of restful sleep means I need more caffeine. "I'm going to live."

"What's with you? It's not like you went out last night."

"My dreams are back," I say. I told Lucy about them after my strange encounter with the tattoo lady. She laughed along with me. But she doesn't look so amused now. "What?"

"Nothing. It's just kind of weird they came back." She's smiling, but it's not real.

I grin to relieve her worry. "Maybe I'm about to meet the mystery man in calculus. That would make the class so worth it." I pull the towel off my wet hair as Lucy frowns. I add, "Dude, I'm not serious. That woman was cray."

She shakes her head. "It's not that. I'm just dreading Professor Gum."

"Don't." I drag a comb through my hair as I glance in the mirror. Drops of moisture drip on my shirt to spread. "I'll get you through this, and then you'll never have to do math again."

"If you do, I'll love you forever."

A button clicks as I turn on my blow-dryer, and hot air blasts at me. As I style my hair, I revisit my dream and burn the man's face to memory. I'm not sure why I believe it, but I'm positive I'll see him some day. And when I do, I want to be sure it's the man of my dreams, because I've got some questions. Desire flickers in my belly. *Lots of questions.*

My first one is, why am I here? As a female engineering major, I had a nice selection of colleges I could have attended, and everyone was shocked when I picked UMO. Sure, their curriculum is a good one, but it's not the best. And then there was the issue of my parents' alma mater. Thankfully, my two sisters decided to fulfill that obligation by attending the small exclusive school a few hours south of here.

Silence comforts my ears when I turn off the blow-dryer and fluff my hair. I grab my mascara, and the smooth wand handle is slippery in my fingers as I twist it open. I recall the day I toured campus as a prospective student. I felt an overwhelming sense of peace being here. As soon as we started to drive away, a dull ache filled me, and when I got home I experienced pain similar to what I felt when my dog died. A depression that disappeared the day I arrived last fall. *What the heck was that about?*

I wiggle into my jeans. Yeah, dream guy. I'm going to need some answers when we meet. Lucy breaks into my thoughts with her words. "Five minutes. We need to go."

I rush to finish getting ready and hop out the door as I pull on my boot. Lucy is walking briskly ahead of me, and I have to jog to catch up.

Once we get outside, the winter air bites through my thin shirt, and I yank my jacket shut and cross my arms over it to keep it that way. "You're really nervous about this, aren't you?"

Lucy glares at me. "You don't get it. Math is my own

personal hell. Calculus might as well be a lost language nobody can decipher." She huffs. "I hate being stupid."

"You're not stupid. Seventy-five percent of the population doesn't get high-level math either. I think that makes you normal." *Unlike your strange roommate who believes dream guys exist.*

The whine of a band saw carries through the cold air, and hammering echoes. A dorm is being renovated, and I glance over at it.

"Really?"

A black Jeep pulls up and stops. "Yes, really." My words come out automatically because I'm focused on the vehicle as if it's hypnotized me. My tattoo is most definitely throbbing now, and when the car door opens, I gasp at the large man who climbs out. I stop in my tracks. *It's him.*

My roommate asks, "What are you doing?"

"I know that guy."

"We don't have time for this." Lucy's grip on my arm is so tight, it might leave a mark as she yanks at me.

I glance at her. She's right. Professor Gum is known for punishing students who are late. I let her lead me toward the lecture hall as I glance over my shoulder. *Dream guy, I'll be back later.* Because the tattoo woman was right. You are real.

CHAPTER 14

Isabelle

I CAN'T GET Luke Robichaux out of my head. I crave his body more than I crave the thrill of a fresh hookup. The very idea that I might be falling for him strikes fear in my heart. The last thing I want is to be influenced by something as ridiculous as love. The only person who will get that sort of power over me will be my true mate, and it's not Luke Robichaux.

I toss a sweater over my shoulder, and it lands on the floor behind me with a soft thump. A light rap on my door makes me growl out, "Come in." I know it's Tristan by the sound of his chuckle.

"Cranky doesn't suit you."

"Yeah? How about full-blown bitchy?" I shove the drawer in the bureau shut, and the wooden furniture shudders as it slams. "When we finally have money again, I'm going to have a decent wardrobe."

"I'm sure my Annie would lend you something."

"*Your* Annie?" Of course I knew that, because even the deaf could have heard their mating this morning. My toes curl as the recollection of my own screaming last night floods my brain. I hold my head and close my eyes as if I can squeeze all traces of Luke from memory. I let out a roar.

"Whoa. What's wrong, Izzy?" Tristan's large hands land on my shoulders, and I open my eyes to his concerned face.

"I'm going to Kick It with Carly to meet with Ian about a job, and I haven't got anything suitable to wear." Kick It is a martial arts studio that caters to werebear while maintaining a front for the human population.

My brother squints at me. "Why don't you tell me what's really bothering you?"

My pulse quickens. No way can I tell Tristan I'm struggling with my attraction for Luke. "How do you know when you've met your true mate?"

"Are you jealous of me and Annie?"

Maybe, but that's not my problem. "No. More like curious." I force out a laugh. "I want to be that happy someday." I pull out my favorite long-sleeved T-shirt and decide that it's dressed up enough for a gym.

"It's like you'd expect." Tristan picks up the sweater I threw earlier and begins to fold it. "The person invades your every thought, and you don't mind. You want to be with them even if you just said goodbye." He sets the garment on the bed and reaches for another. His eyes sparkle. He pauses as if he's remembering something. "You find yourself wanting to do little things for them to see a smile." My brother grins. "And the moment after you've said goodbye, you begin to count the minutes until you'll see them again."

He's just described what I would imagine is his idea of hell. But when Tristan rakes his hand through his hair without worry of what it'll do to his perfectly combed locks, I'm gobsmacked. My brother is in love. I was sure that wasn't possible, even with a true mate attraction. "That must have been some amazing sex you had his morning." Mating brings the bond to the forefront, and when the bite happens, the couple's fate is sealed. *You didn't!* "Did you bite Annie?"

Tristan sits on my bed and grabs a pair of my jeans. "I'm always amazing." He zips them up and snaps the waistband shut. "But no, I didn't bite her." The denim snaps as he flicks them out in the air to release the wrinkles. "I *can't* bite her. That would change everything, and I need to be in control."

I snort. "Really? Because the way you're acting right now, I don't think you are able to help yourself."

He glares at me, and I see the cold, calculating brother I've come to know. He sets down the pants, and the crease is razor sharp from his precision. Tristan says, "Make no mistake. Mating with Annie hasn't changed anything."

"If you say so. But love wouldn't be such a bad thing, you know." I slide into loose jeans that hang low on my waist. "For either of us."

Tristan comes toward me and grips my arms. "Izzy, you are loved. By me." He pulls me against his chest.

"And I'm loved by you. That's enough."

I used to believe that it was. But since we got here, he's been pulling away. I'm watching my brother struggle with wanting the one thing all werebear want–a true mate. Even though he knows it can't be. My heart aches in sympathy that the love Tristan and I crave is the very thing he must sacrifice.

I step back before tears begin to burn in my eyes. Tristan has been strong for me all my life, and it's time I returned the favor. "It's not enough, and you know it."

He grabs my hand and grips it tight. "It needs to be."

I shake my head. "You do your part, and I'll do mine." I force a wink at him. "Because doing Luke Robichaux isn't half bad."

Annie calls up to us from the kitchen to announce lunch. The silly grin of love returns to Tristan's face. The familiar sense of dread is heavy in my gut when I remember the day we discovered he and Annie were true mates. I knew then it changed everything, no matter how insistent Tristan was that it wouldn't.

I watch my brother leave with a lightness in his step I didn't know he possessed. I want to grab him and tell him to protect his heart. And I wonder how he's going to manage when the love of his life discovers what we've done. Funny how a deal with the devil seems like a wise choice when faced with the threat of extinction. But it's not so funny when the promises you make present you with a fresh new hell. I drag my hair up in a high ponytail, and the elastic snaps as I attach it. I gaze into the mirror at my high cheekbones and strong jaw. *Izzy, find your strength, girl.* Because Tristan's days of protecting me are over. Now it's my turn, because the future of the clan depends on me.

CHAPTER 15

Annie

T HE KNIFE CLINKS against glass as I scoop out mustard for a sandwich. The scent of Tristan floats toward me, and a smile creeps on my face. Two large hands slap down on the counter as large arms trap me. I glance at the sleeves of his shirt that are rolled up on his muscular forearms. I recall how it was only a few days ago that the naked version of my mate did this, and I lean back to wiggle my butt in his groin.

His voice rumbles in my ear. "I thought you had to work."

"I did. But I discovered they didn't need me." The girls who work for me in the retail shop are quite capable, and I couldn't focus, so I decided to come back to my distraction.

Tristan moves hair from my neck and places a kiss on it below my earlobe. "I do." He nips at me, and the scrape of his teeth makes my spine tingle. I want his bite with an intensity that almost consumes me.

I lean my head back and offer my neck up to him. He

suckles my nape as his hands cover my breasts. "What if I bent you over the counter and took you right here? Would you scream for me?"

I whisper, "Yes." He presses his palms hard against my torso as he drags his hands down. One stops at my hip, and the other cups my mound. Denim is a thick barrier between our flesh, and I whimper. I don't know what's holding me back, because it's normal for new mates to spend weeks screwing any free chance they get. But most try not to do it in front of their families while they eat lunch. I grind my butt against his groin, and his erection tempts me to throw all social graces to the wind. I stop myself before I have to live with a long-running family joke about a meat counter.

I turn to face Tristan. "Laundry room. Now." I grab his hand and tug him along behind me as I lead the way to the small area that doubles as a bathroom. When we enter, Tristan shuts the door behind him. The lock snicks shut, and he grins. I have a long counter for folding clothes, and it's just the right height for his previous idea.

He reaches for my hips and turns me around so that he's behind me. Nudging me forward, he presses against my bottom as he reaches for my waistband. "How close are you, love?"

My chest is heaving with short breaths as he pulls roughly, and my zipper rips open. "Very." Denim abrades my skin as he yanks my jeans down to mid-thigh. A cool draft travels between my legs, and I let my pants fall to my ankles and step out, but it does nothing to tamp down the fire of my lust. Tristan pushes my shoulder so I'll bend over. My breasts flatten on the cool laminate counter top, and I splay my arms out as the clash of a belt buckle sounds behind me while he undoes his pants.

He grips my hips hard and thrusts into me quickly. He hisses, "Dripping-wet ready." A growl escapes from him, and he slams into me with force. I brace my hands against the wall and pump my hips into him. I want him to be deeper and say, "Fill me. Make me feel it."

My mate's fingers dig into my flesh, and I'm sure he'll leave bruises. Our coupling is fast, and the moment my channel flexes with my release, Tristan's low rumbling in his throat tells me he isn't far behind. When he finishes, his trembling body slumps over me, and he squeezes me tight enough to hurt. He relaxes a bit, and teeth prick at my earlobe when he whispers, "It's time."

I nod, and the fabric of my blouse rips as he strips it from my shoulder to plunge his bear fangs into my flesh. The sensation is like an orgasm on steroids, and I shatter completely as I cry out his name.

He growls, "Mine," as he thrusts into me again.

My pleasure has barely retreated before the wave comes back another time. Once it crests, I fall with it and say, "Yes. I'm yours."

Tristan groans as he explodes in me, and his words reach all the way to my heart when he says, "And I'm yours."

My legs are like jelly as I use the counter for support under my mate's heavy weight. He laps at my blood and heals my wound. The area is sensitive, and each stroke of his tongue sends tiny aftershocks through me as he finishes. Hair is stuck to my neck, and he plucks it off my sweat-slicked skin to kiss me lightly. He repeats his earlier words as if he's making sure we both heard. "I'm yours, Annie." A sigh comes from him, and his voice is low enough only my bear ears can detect it. "Forever."

My mate. My true mate scoops me up and lifts me to sit on the counter. He stands between my legs and palms the back of my head as he gazes into my eyes. "I love you, Annie. No matter what happens, I will always love and protect you."

I'm lost in the icy-blue depth of his eyes. They trap me in his love, and I say, "I love you too, Tristan."

He kisses me gently, and we hold on to each other as if we don't dare let go. I realize we have both found a savior. The De Rozier alpha now has a new place for his kingdom, and I get the family I've always craved.

Once we've recovered and I change into a new shirt, we emerge to go back to the kitchen. Carly and Isabelle are at the table. Carly has a smirk when she asks, "Hungry?"

Tristan hugs my shoulders with an arm as if he's protecting me. "I think we satisfied our hunger. Now what's for lunch?"

Isabelle's eyes are hard as she stares at Tristan, and I wonder why she's angry. Her chair almost topples over when she stands abruptly, and she moves to leave the kitchen. But Tristan grabs her arm. "Izzy! We need to talk."

She yanks it away and spits out, "*Nothing's changed.* Wrong, brother dear. Everything just did."

PART 2

CHAPTER 16

Isabelle

I START TO run before the shift happens. Fabric shreds as I explode out of my clothing, and the sound is satisfying. Hell, I didn't even take off my shoes. I'm sure the carnage I create will appall Annie's sensibilities. But I don't care, because she's not my favorite person right now. My legs surge with energy as my large feet pound in a frantic cadence. The memories of Tristan and Annie calling out each other's names in the throes of passion echo in my head, and my blood boils over.

When I get to the trees, I smash my shoulder into a pine. Wood splinters, but the tree doesn't fall, so I stop. I'm beyond furious right now. A loud crack sounds as I smash the tree again, and it crashes into a few more. Plowing through the woods, I swing my front legs out to either side as if I'm blazing a trail. Branches fall like rain. Birds take flight. A startled deer races across my path. I snarl at it. *That's right, Bambi, be afraid. Be very afraid.* Everyone and everything better get out of my way.

"Isabelle!" Tristan's trying to communicate with me

telepathically, and I thought I'd blocked him out. But because he's the alpha of my clan, he can get through anyway. He's also the main reason I'm so enraged. Fucking true mates; it ruins everything.

My lips curl up as I growl. He better not alpha order me. He said Annie being his true mate wouldn't be a problem. He said he could handle it. He said he wasn't going to seal the true mate bond by biting Annie. *Fucking liar!* I scream across the telepathic airwaves.

I'm panting, and the damage I've done to my body has caught up with me as I limp in a slow walk. I glance down to discover red streaks of blood staining my fur. My legs are tired, and I slow down some more. I slap at a tree, but it barely moves as my anger lessens and my muscles weaken with exhaustion.

My brother bit Annie, his true mate, and now they're bonded for life. They'll want to live and breathe each other. While that's good for the first stage of our plan, he's never going to be able to betray her for the second part. The part where we take over the Le Roux kingdom for our own.

I turn and thud to the ground to inspect my injuries. Glancing at the wreckage I created, I notice more than blood splatters on the snow. I'm gushing it.

I gaze at my front paws to find they're shredded. Further inspection makes me notice a large gash in my belly where the blood is coagulating. I'll live. A stick is stuck in my back leg, and I yank it out. *Bloody hell!* It hurts like a mother, but my pun makes me chuckle. I am a bloody mess. My body shakes as my laughter becomes uncontrollable. I'm so screwed now that Tristan has abandoned me. Tears begin to flow freely from my eyes.

Pain radiates through my injuries as I flop onto my back and stare up at the sky. It's overcast again, and I wonder why we came here. All it does is snow, and I long for the crystal blue skies and blinding sun of the Arctic. My brother has found the love of his life, and no matter what he says, I've lost him. *To a freaking wimpy black bear.* Our mother will be furious when she finds out. Not that she can do anything about it now that Tristan is our alpha, but technically she's still the prima.

I snort with force, and snot sprays over me as I imagine my mother's reaction to losing prima status to Annie. I laugh again, because the evil bitch is finally going to be powerless. It's about time.

"Izzy. I can smell you. I'm on my way."

My brother, the savior. He's always been there to pick up the pieces from our abusive parents. And myself. The steady cadence of his feet tells me he's not far away. I lie and wait.

Polar bears are regular bears to the tenth power. Our bodies are bigger, our sense of smell is so great we can detect a seal more than twenty miles away, and we can communicate for almost a thousand miles instead of fifty or so. We also heal faster than other bear, and by the time Tristan is hovering over me, blocking out the sky, my paws are almost normal.

"Izzy, you scared me."

I swipe my claws across his face, and he stumbles back as I sit up. Blood drips down his snout as he asks, *"Feel better?"*

"Not really. But I am over the urge to kill you."

"It's not what you think."

I huff. *"Is that like some male DNA thing to pull out those words whenever you want someone to brush aside the facts?"*

"No. But—"

"I heard you. Everyone heard you. You bit Annie and sealed your bond. What am I supposed to think?"

"That I'd never leave you. And that I know what I'm doing."

"You're lying to yourself if you believe that. I knew the day would come when I'd lose you to a mate." The scratches I gave him have healed, and I know most of my cuts have, too, so I stand. I pick up some snow and rub at the blood stains on my fur. But what I need is the river.

"Izzy, it won't be like that. Annie and I want you to live with us."

"I need to swim. Go back and be with Annie."

He places a paw on my shoulder, and I shrug it off. I trudge through the snow toward the river.

Tristan follows behind me, but I take a little satisfaction in his guilt.

When we get to the water, I dive in and let the coolness soothe my achy body. Tristan sits on the bank to watch. I duck under and swim along the bottom. I'm used to depths so vast that blackness is usually underneath me, and my heart aches as I miss my homeland. It hits me that now I've got nothing. The one true thing in my life no longer belongs to me; Tristan belongs to Annie.

When I get out and shake, Tristan approaches me and nuzzles my neck. I glance over at the magnificent bear he is. In human form, he's got pale blond hair and icy blue eyes, just like me. But right now his fur has a faint orange cast that comes from his obsession with sweet potatoes. Nobody has told him. I used to think it worked for his cover story, but now his cover's blown. Annie will see who he really is, because it can't be helped. I say, *"You're eating too much carotene, and your fur is orange. They laugh at you for it."*

He glances down and lets out an annoyed growl as I lead the way home.

CHAPTER 17

Tori

THE PAWPRINT TATTOO on the fleshy part of me that covers my hip is throbbing, and I squirm in my chair to alleviate the pressure of my jeans on it. My mind has been flooded with the images of the hot guy I dream about. Which wouldn't be a bad thing if I weren't supposed to be focused on a calculus lecture.

I force myself to hear the professor's words and follow along with his calculations projected on a big screen for all the students to see. It's no use. The image of my dream guy's perfectly formed pecs and the dusting of hair on them flashes before me, blocking out numbers, letters, and lines.

When I shift again in my seat, my roommate Lucy pokes me with her pen. I glance at her, and she shoots an angry look back. She's depending on me to get her through this class, but that's not going to go so well for us if I'm on the verge of failing, too. I pull out my phone and break Professor Gum's no-texting rule, which he announced less than ten minutes ago to send one to Lucy.

Don't worry, I can do this in my sleep.

"Miss Text-a-lot!"

I look up in horror as people in the class turn to figure out who he's looking at. The professor glares at me. "Out."

"But—"

"No excuses. Go."

Shame burns my ears, and I grab my things to leave. When Lucy catches my eye I think she might cry. I mouth. "Sorry." But the truth is I'm not. Because this means I can go find the guy that's causing my distraction.

On our way to class, we walked by a dorm renovation, and my tattoo was pulsing like mad as if it's some kind of hot-guy detector. And when I glanced over at the men working, the one who got out of a Jeep looked suspiciously like the guy I dream about. Leaving the lecture early means I might be able to find him again.

My footsteps echo in the stairway as I jog down and shove the metal door open to leave the building. It slams shut behind me as cold wind whips my hair around my face. I didn't take the time to put my coat on before I got outside, and I should do it now. But I'm afraid I might miss the man in my dreams, so I continue to run instead.

My backpack's contents rattle as it bounces on my back, and I head toward the dorm. When I get around the corner, I see the Jeep. *He's still here.* I slow to a walk, and icy air burns in my lungs, making me wonder why I'm so compelled that I've become frantic. Sweat is damp on my skin, and the wind sends a chill through me. When I reach the car, I stop to remove my pack and retrieve my jacket.

There is an image on the door of the vehicle, and I memorize the pine-tree logo that reads Bear Mountain Tree Farm. My zipper hums as I tug it up to my chin, and I bend down to pick up my pack again. When I stand, I notice a man coming my way. He's huge, with broad shoulders and narrow hips. The temperature is cold with the wind chill today, but apparently he's warm enough to keep his flannel-lined jean jacket open.

As he gets closer, there's no doubt he's the man in my dreams. He frowns as he approaches me, and I realize I'm staring at him with my mouth open as if I'm mesmerized. I kind of am, because the things this guy does in my imagination are pretty amazing. I recover my wits and say, "Hi."

"Is there something I can help you with?"

He has no idea who I am. I guess the dreams are a one-way thing. "This is going to sound really weird, but I think I know you."

The guy shakes his head as his brow remains furrowed. "I don't think so."

My body hums in his proximity, and I step closer. I take a deep breath to inhale the scent of pine mixed with his faint musk, and I almost moan at the pleasure it brings. I step even closer so that I'm in his personal bubble. He crosses his arms as if they're a barrier, and I gaze up at him to say, "I'm Tori."

He's not amused and steps back as he asks, "Is this

some kind of sorority initiation thing?"

The need to touch him overwhelms me, and I reach out. But he retreats as if I have a communicable disease. "No. I've—" *You've what, Tori? You can't tell him you have sex dreams about him. He'll think you're a fruit loop.* "I'm sorry. I really thought I knew you. But I guess not."

"We've never met. Now if you'd be so kind as to move out of my way, I need to leave."

I take a few steps away from the Jeep. I don't want him to go, and I grasp at a straw to deter him. "So you must be the boss."

The door of the car opens with a groan, and he leans an arm on it as he glances over at me. "Something like that."

Desperation sets in, and words I haven't formed into coherency tumble out of my mouth. "Sweet. You should use me as an intern. I'm a super-smart engineering student and need to line something up for the summer. I've got references, and everyone will tell you I'm…" I stop, because his eyes are crinkled up as if he's about to laugh at me.

Heat rises to my cheeks, and I shake my head. "I'm so sorry." I start to walk backward. "I'm just going to—" I step into a pothole and stumble before I fall on my butt. Sharp pain shoots up my spine. "Ouch!"

The man towers over me. "Are you okay?"

I gaze into the blue eyes I recall from my dreams. "I think so."

He reaches out a hand, and I grab on as he hoists me

up with enough strength that he might as well have lifted me. The heat of his fingers burns my chilled skin, and I grip him tight so he won't let go yet. The oddest sensation surges through me, and I whisper, "Do you feel that?"

The guy yanks his hand back. "You're a strange girl."

I gasp as our connection breaks and stare down at my palm. I glance back up at him. His eyes are hard as if he's angry, and adrenaline spikes in me. Like he's the one that has a right to be mad. I blurt out, "Look. You're the one invading my dreams like a creeper. So why don't you just stop and then you'll never have to see me again? Okay?"

He tilts his head and squints at me as he bends down to retrieve the backpack I dropped. "Dreams, huh?"

I yank the bag from him. "Yes, dreams. And those stupid dreams made me get a tattoo. *Me.* The girl who cries when she gets a splinter got a tattoo. Do you know what that means?"

"So why aren't you crying now? That fall had to have hurt more than a splinter."

I huff. "Unbelievable. I'm exaggerating. The point is you're making me crazy, and you think I'm the one who's strange. Geeze." I cross my arms and glare at him.

His face breaks into a smile. "I'm teasing you."

"Oh." I take a deep breath. "So do you know who I am?"

"No. But I do have an idea what's going on."

Relief washes over me, and I let out a big sigh. "Thank god."

He slides into his car, and I actually stomp my foot

because I think he's going to drive off without telling me a thing. "Don't you dare drive off on me."

He pops his head back out of the Jeep with a slip of paper and a pen. He's smiling when he hands it to me. "Give me your number, and I'll let you know when I get this all sorted out."

I frown. "What, you don't own a phone?"

He taunts me. "What, you don't know how to write?"

I roll my eyes and scribble my name and number down. "You're kind of annoying, you know that?"

Now he smiles. "It's part of my charm. But don't worry. You'll be rid of me soon."

My hands are freezing, and after I hand him the note, I shove them in my jacket pockets. "Thanks."

The man reaches for his door handle and says, "Goodbye, Tori."

"Bye."

The Jeep door slams shut, and the engine roars as he turns it on. I step back and watch him back out before turning to walk to my dorm. Sadness wraps around me as if I just said goodbye to a boyfriend who broke up with me. I turn to watch the Jeep as he drives away. When it turns the corner and is no longer visible, I sigh, because he was so much better in my dreams.

CHAPTER 18

Annie

T HE WAFFLE IRON creaks as I lower the top over the batter I just poured. I turn to the man who has just entered the kitchen. "Keith." I walk over and hug Brady's best friend, someone who's practically a brother to me. I hold him a little longer than is normal, as if I can take some of his pain away with my touch. And because I remember how he did the same for me when my true mate died a few years ago. "I'm glad you're here."

"Thanks. I've missed your breakfasts."

"Well, dig in, before Brady eats it all."

A plate clatters on the table as Mother sets it down and walks over to hug Keith, too. "So good to see you again, dear."

When they step apart, Keith says, "Donna, I need you to do something for me."

"Of course. What is it?"

He walks over, and coffee splashes into a mug as he pours. "There's a young girl at Orono that was called and is dreaming about me. Can you cancel it or something?"

Almost two years ago, our clan put out a call to bring in women of werebear descent to bear children for us. Mother says, "Oh dear." Keith's jaw flexes when Mother sighs, and she continues. "There isn't any way to cancel the call. Goodness, she has to have been dreaming about you for a while."

Sierra places bacon on her plate and lifts a piece up as she says, "Wow. That's a long time to be having those dreams."

Carly's already at the table with her food and says, "Oh my god. Are you talking about Tori?"

Keith nods. "You know her?"

"Yeah, she came in a while back for a tattoo. I expected she'd be back to find out more about her dream guy, but she never returned. I was going to call her to follow up."

"So like the rest of you human women, she came here because she was dreaming about her potential mate?" He glances over at Sierra. "How did I get two of you?"

Sierra came here with Carly to mate with Keith, but their relationship didn't work out, which was a good thing, because she ended up being Ashton's true mate. She bumps him with her hip. "You're just that hot."

Keith smiles at her. "I'm also that old. Tori's a kid."

Brady teases, "You're the older man. I hear that's sexy for young girls."

Carly hits his arm. "Perv."

"Exactly." Keith frowns. "Besides the fact I have no interest in another mate, I sure don't want to hook up with a child."

Silence falls, and I imagine we're all thinking about his mate Taylor and her tragic death. I jump in to fill the void. "We'll just have to ask Kimi what to do. This situation is just wrong." Kimi is our medicine woman and the one that put out the call that made human women of werebear descent start dreaming about eligible Le Roux men. Some of them were more open than others and came to us.

Sierra says, "She's a freshman at Orono. I wonder if maybe Tori didn't do anything about the call for so long because she wasn't legal?"

Mother says, "Could be." She breaks off a piece of blueberry muffin. "Don't worry Keith, we'll sort this out."

"Thank you." He sets his plate of food down with a thump and pulls a piece of paper out of his back pocket. "Here's her number."

My mother takes it and reads it before folding it up and setting it down. "I'll bet one of Delia's twins would be suitable for her. They're the youngest in the clan." Carly chuckles and Mom asks, "What?"

"You really should consider a career in matchmaking."

She smiles over her teacup at us. "I have a gift. Just ask Annie about the polar bear I found."

My cheeks flush, and I'm sure my smile looks foolish. "You do get points for that one."

Keith says, "I heard Tristan is your true mate. That's great." He reaches over and puts his hand over mine.

"You deserve this."

"Thanks." I remember how I was sure life was over when Kyle died, and nobody could have ever made me believe someday I'd be giddy in love again. I hope my second chance at lifelong happiness gives Keith hope. He deserves it, too.

Mother clears her throat to get our attention. Even though when Brady married Carly, Mother stepped down as prima, she still runs our weekly meetings. My sister-in-law is a smart woman, because she figured out that the best way to keep Mother happy and helpful is to let her feel as if she has some control over the family. She says, "That brings us to the most important order of business this morning—the land we're gifting to the De Rozier clan."

Brady says, "The papers are begin drawn up, and the De Roziers will soon own the one thousand acres that surround Crystal Lake."

I reach out and touch Brady's arm. "Thank you."

My brother's face is serious when he says, "I do have one stipulation, though. While I realize the true mate bond should be security enough, I put your name on the deed."

I nod as I wonder how Tristan will feel about that. But I suppose if it's not common knowledge, it shouldn't matter. We'll never separate.

Sierra says, "Hey, I heard about Isabelle's temper tantrum the other day. That girl's got issues. Did she ever apologize for it?"

I answer, "Yes. She went out the next day and cleaned up her mess, but she definitely left a mark."

"More like a new trail," says Carly. She shrugs. "But with a few more trees down, it does give us a direct route to the river."

Sierra says, "Still, that's a pretty severe reaction to your brother sealing a true mate bond."

Mother shakes her head. "She's had a difficult up-bringing. Her parents weren't known to be warm and fuzzy. I think she felt abandoned."

I get it. I remember the loss I experienced when Brady and Carly discovered they were true mates. Brady had been the shoulder I leaned on when my husband died. "Then I'll just have to do what I can to make sure she still gets time with Tristan."

"I think anger-management classes might be a better idea," says Sierra as she rolls her eyes to the sky.

Ashton says, "Or maybe she needs a more rigorous workout schedule. I could use her as a warrior."

Brady's jaw is tight in alpha mode as he nods. "Train her. But I'm not sure I trust her just yet. Something about that girl is off."

"Agreed," says Carly. "I can't put my finger on it, but I don't trust her, either."

I think about her almost nightly drunk hook-ups. She's definitely self-destructive as a reaction to some-thing, and I wonder what it could be. But I know she's in good hands with Ashton. He used to be a Navy SEAL and has seen things I can't even imagine. I've got no doubt if anyone can get through to Isabelle, it's Ash.

I capture his gaze and say, "Help her."

He nods in response.

CHAPTER 19

Isabelle

THE LE ROUX act as if tearing through the forest in a rage makes me crazy. They have no idea it's standard learned behavior for a polar bear with a temper. They should be grateful they didn't know me as a child. It took years for me to learn to control my anger, and I'm proud of myself for not attacking Tristan, or even worse, Annie.

I stretch my arms over my head, and a lingering soreness is still present in the limb I shattered. Nothing I can't handle, though. Ashton is across the gym, and I watch him approach me. His legs are the size of tree trunks, and I bet he works out for hours every day.

I'm glad it's him, because I still have some resentment I need to work out, and Ian, the guy who runs Kick It, isn't bear enough for my strength. Even though Ashton isn't a polar bear, he's got finesse on his side. He'll know how to save himself if I get out of control.

I bounce on my feet to warm up my muscles and recheck my hand wraps. Ashton nods at me, and I say, "Hey."

He walks over to a set of shelves and grabs two jump ropes. I reach into the air to grab the one he throws toward me, and the handles are smooth in my hand as I prepare to do what he says. But he doesn't speak. Instead Ashton starts jumping across from me, so I copy his movements.

"You don't talk?"

A small smile forms on his face.

"Good. I can do enough for both of us."

"If you're talking, then you're not working hard enough." He speeds up and changes his movements.

Got it, tough guy. I match him step for step, and the slapping of our ropes on the floor is paired perfectly. At the point my eyes begin to burn from sweat dripping into them, I notice Ashton is breathing easily, while I've started to pant from the exertion. Damn, I'm impressed. A half hour later, my lungs are screaming from lack of oxygen, and I'm close to passing out. But I've never backed down from a challenge, so I keep going.

Ashton stops and nods toward the large punching bag. He executes a five-movement drill and steps away. "Fifteen minutes."

I nod. The no-talking thing is contagious. I've only just caught my breath when he says, "Faster." I blow out a burst of air and pick up my pace. Pain radiates through my hands with each strike, and I'm at the point at which I would stop if I were on my own when Ashton barks out, "Harder."

My growl sounds in annoyance, and I punch with

more force. Now the agony of impact radiates through my arms, and I let it drive me. Tristan's face comes to mind, and I imagine hitting his nose as my growl becomes a constant rumble in my throat. *You left me.* I drive my fist hard, and white-hot agony races to my shoulder. *You said you'd always take care of me.*

Ashton's loud order startles me. "Stop." I step back and bend over my thighs. Sweat drips on the mat, and I gasp for air as I recover. Blue eyes cut into me as he leans down to get my attention. "Kicks."

I stand up and watch his progression. When he steps away, I go in with renewed energy. This time I remember my father. When my foot slaps at the leather bag, the sound brings me back to being a small girl, and my cheek stings with the memory of my father's hand. I want to laugh, because that was for a minor infraction like being in the same room if he was annoyed.

I begin to kick harder as I recall the beatings. The ones I learned to take instead of fighting back. But I got my retribution, as any polar bear in my clan would tell you. The girls feared me, while the boys learned to stay out of my way. Only Tristan could get through to me when the rages hit.

Drops of salty moisture fly as I spin and deliver kicks faster and harder. My breathing is so labored that it sounds as if I'm gasping, and my chest hurts. I pour on all I've got, and the bag splits with a loud tear from the impact of a kick. I don't stop, and each one of my blows pulverizes the stuffing.

Ashton commands me to stop. He eyes the carnage of the punching bag. His gaze is intense as he says, "We'll need to order a few more of those."

It would be funny if I thought he was cracking a joke. But he's not, and I nod in reply. He walks us over to the weights, and I catch a glimpse of Ian cleaning up my mess.

My arms and legs are like jelly, but my rage has subsided. I focus on controlled movements as Ashton takes me through a circuit. Partway through the second round, he leaves me. My brother may have ditched me for Annie, but I'm a survivor. I smile as I formulate my next move.

Luke.

Ian approaches me. I glance at the strong, sexy man in front of me. Yup. My rage is definitely gone if I'm thinking about sex. He says, "Ash had to leave for a bit, but he asked me to work on some combinations with you."

I smile sweetly. "I'd like that."

Ian's definitely a flirt. "We're going to work on grace." He winks at me. "Think lover, not fighter."

He's a strong contrast to Ashton, and I grin back. "Can do."

Ian walks me through a combination and asks me to focus on placement and smooth transitions. He says, "I want to hear the faintest of taps when you make contact with the leather. If it slaps, you're striking too hard."

I dance around the bag and focus on fluidity. Luke's careful hands come to mind, and I imagine I'm mimicking his touch. My skin flushes with the memory, and I'm grateful I've sweat so much that my musk masks the scent of my arousal. Ian calls out praise and direction.

Once I've grasped the grace, Ian instructs me to take it up a notch and use a bit of force. This time I punch and kick with enough power to make noise but not enough that I lose smoothness.

When Ian calls for a break, I say, "That does feel like dancing. Thanks."

"I like to think of fighting like relationships."

I shake my head.

"No," says Ian. "Seriously. Think about it. It's more than the sex, it's the love and caring that goes with it that makes it the love real. Same thing with fighting. You need to mix the power with grace, agility and speed."

I nod at him as we make our way to the water cooler. It makes sense. If I want a relationship with Luke, I'm going to need more than great sex. And I'm going to need to give more than that, too. Perhaps it's time to go after what I need now that Tristan has replaced me as his number one. I take a deep breath and let it out slowly. My anger is gone, and what's left is an empty shell ready to be filled with more than rage. And maybe Luke Robichaux is the one that can help.

CHAPTER 20

Tori

Y EAH, SO MY dream guy never called. And he's still a nightly visitor who makes me look forward to sleep. Now that I've seen him in real life, the dreams are even more intense. I swear I can smell him and feel his burning touch. But I can't live like this forever, so I've decided I needed to do something.

After Googling Bear Mountain Tree Farm, I discovered the headquarters and the lumber mill. Based on the scent of pine that was on the guy, I guess he works at the lumber mill. I would have called to find out, but he never gave me a name. I glance down at the speedometer of my car and ease my foot off the gas pedal, because I'm going way too fast. My stomach flips over as I begin to question my sanity.

My phone calls out my next turn, and I realize it's the road to the lumber mill. I take a deep breath and hope my dream guy doesn't turn me away. At least this time I thought about what I'm going to say so a stream of babble doesn't spout out of my mouth. Now to find him.

As I approach the parking lot, my palms get sweaty, and my tattoo begins to throb. *He's here.* When I park, my eyes fall shut for a moment as the memory of his lips on my neck floods my mind. I tingle in response but shake my head to clear my thoughts. This guy is so not interested in me that way.

Loud bangs and shouts sound as I head toward a tractor trailer that contains logs. A man is in a vehicle with a long-armed claw that squeaks as it unloads the wood and places it on a moving chute. A guy in a plaid jacket jumps down from the cab of the truck that is being unloaded and notices me. He smiles, and I don't miss his quick scan of my body. I don't usually turn heads like thin girls do, but this male clearly appreciates the way I look judging by the low noise he makes under his breath.

"Hello, sweetheart. Can I help you?"

"I'm looking for the boss."

"Are you now? Which one?"

Oh boy. "Um, the guy who's really tall with dark hair and blue eyes."

The man grins. "Darn, my eyes are brown. You must want Keith."

I smile back, because while I don't think he's anyone's boss, I appreciate the flirting. "That sounds right. Do you know where I can find him?"

"Try the office." He points to a door. "Right through there and to the right. Can't miss it."

I pull a piece of hair out of my mouth that the wind blew into my face and tuck it behind my ear. "Thanks."

The main door of the building is heavy, clear glass, and I yank hard to get it open. When it shuts behind me, the noise outside is muffled, and I walk slowly along the dark-gray industrial carpet. My heart beats against my chest as I try to remember what I was going to say. When I turn right, the hallway opens up to a reception area, and past it, a door is ajar.

I find my courage and throw my shoulders back as I approach. He's sitting at the desk, and keys click as he types on a computer. My knuckles rap on the door to get his attention. The guy looks up in confusion and blinks to focus.

"Hi."

He stands up as his face relaxes. "Tori."

My face heats up, because my body betrays me with its sexual urges. His eyes are so blue that it's like staring into the sky, and I lose my train of thought. Breaking away from his gaze, I focus on his chin. "I hadn't heard from you and thought maybe you lost my number. I would have called, but you didn't give me your name."

Unfortunately his chin is too close to his lips, and I lick mine in the memory of what he tasted like in last night's dream.

The man glances at me, and his eyes are squinted before he relaxes them with a sigh. "I'm sorry. I'll bet this is hard for you."

I nod. He's not angry, but his brow is furrowed a bit as if something's wrong. "I shouldn't have come here," I say as I start to back away.

"No. It's okay." He comes out from behind his desk. "I'm Keith. Do you want some milk and cookies?"

Seriously? Does he think I'm seven? But a cookie does sound good. "Sure."

"Right this way." Keith leads me back toward the hall, and we continue straight to go past it. He pulls open a door to a large room and lets me enter first. It appears to be the employee cafeteria, and we walk by round, laminated tables toward a stainless steel machine, where he pours two glasses of milk. I smile when he grabs a cookie and takes a bite. He catches my eye and nods towards the tray of baked goods. I grab one, too.

"Come sit," he says as he walks toward the closest table. We're the only ones in here, and I wonder if he's supposed to be taking a break.

After we're seated, I snap off a bite of my treat and fiddle with it as I say, "If you need to work, we can do this another time."

Keith has a little milk mustache, making him appear younger than he is, judging by his job and the fine lines near his eyes. "Nope. I needed a snack, and you just reminded me."

His words are casual, but he hasn't cracked a smile. Such a serious man. "Okay. Good." I sip my milk to wash down the sugary flavor of cookie.

"Getting rid of your dreams isn't as easy as I thought it was going to be. I'm sorry."

"Oh." I take another sip of my milk and wish I could do something to make him grin. I wait for him to explain more.

He gulps down the rest of his milk and then asks, "Want a tour?"

That's random, but I say, "I'd love one."

I finish my milk, too, and when I'm done, his lips turn up just the slightest as he reaches toward me. I lean in without thinking, and he stops just before he touches me and pulls his hand back quickly. "Ah. You've got a milk mustache."

He does feel this attraction. But why did he stop himself? *Oh, Keith, you shouldn't have done that.* Because even though he didn't touch me, now I know he wants to. I smile as I wipe my mouth with my sleeve. "You do, too."

He copies my movement and grabs my glass as he stands. "C'mon."

He drops the cups in a plastic bin full of dishes on the way out. We leave through a different exit than the one we entered through, and this hallway is industrial, with tile flooring and concrete walls that are lined with hooks and cubbies. An assortment of hard hats is hanging on the wall, and Keith grabs one to inspect it. He holds it out to me. "Try this on."

I place it on my head and cock my hip in a pose. "How do I look?"

The smile he's trying so hard not to crack threatens to escape again. "Cute." He reaches into a cubby and pulls out a hat of his own and two sets of ear-protection headphones. "Here. You'll want these, too."

After we put on the headgear, Keith leads me through a door that opens up to a large warehouse-like space full of machinery. He walks me over to where the chute I saw earlier is carrying in the fresh cut logs and depositing them in a machine that removes the bark. They move on toward a series of saws that cut them into planks. Our headphones don't allow us to communicate other than pointing.

Keith directs me to a small control room, and I'm relieved when we get to remove our ear protection. A computer screen appears to be monitoring the wood planks and rejecting the ones that don't have the right measurements. Keith says, "Do you have any questions about what you've seen so far?"

"What happens to the scraps?"

He answers everything I ask with the patience of someone who finds this as fascinating as I do. When we're done in the control room, he finishes the tour near the trucks being loaded with kiln-dried wood for retail distribution. He brings me back to the hallway, where I return my hard hat. It clatters on the wall as I gush on about the operation, and Keith asks, "Have you always been interested in how things work?"

I nod. "That's why I decided to major in engineering. I was the little girl who took apart her talking doll to see if I could get her to say different things." I grin, recalling my mother's dismay that one of her triplets would rather take her toys apart that use them as intended.

Keith smiles the tiniest bit. "I was that kind of kid,

too." He begins to walk us back toward his office, and our footsteps are muffled again once we hit the carpet.

"Did you major in engineering?"

The heavy door slams behind us, and the silence is almost deafening now that we're in the administrative part of the building. "Yes. I even went to UMO."

My first thought is to ask him when he graduated, but since I got my first smile, I don't want to point out our age difference. "So you're a Black Bear too." The animal is the mascot for the university.

We've stopped at the hallway that leads outside, and his eyes widen for a moment before he furrows his brow. "How much do you know about your dreams?"

"Not much. The woman who gave me my tattoo said I was being called and that the guy in my dreams would want to date me. Only you don't, so…."

He sighs and rakes a hand through his hair. "Tori, I'm twenty-eight. And you're what, eighteen?"

I nod.

Keith lets out a low noise that's almost a growl. "I'm going to figure this out for you." He stares into my eyes, and my body hums with desire I don't want to control. "We aren't right for each other."

I hear the words, but when his lips part and his pupils widen, I don't believe them. He feels our connection, too. I say, "Thanks. Now about that internship. I was serious. I actually need one this semester. Got any openings?"

Keith's shoulders slump in defeat. "I'll make one." He reaches into his shirt pocket and pulls out a card. "Email me the details."

Hope bursts in my heart, and I clutch the card in my hands as I grin. "Thank you. I won't let you down. I promise."

I get a genuine smile this time, and he says, "I know you won't."

CHAPTER 21

Lucy

W HEN TORI TOLD me about her tattoo, I got nervous. I'm sure that's the sign the Le Roux use to
call human women to their clan so they can bear children
and continue the bloodline. Being the daughter of the
Robichaux alpha, I have an in on the politics of the three
clans that make up the Northeast Kingdom, and the
practice of turning humans into werebear didn't sit well
with the other clans when they heard about it.

But once one of the humans turned out to be my
mother's daughter, things changed for Mom. Now Carly
Le Roux is the alpha successor to our clan as well as the
prima for hers. Yeah, that wasn't a big hit with my father.
Not that my mother cheated on him or anything. She had
Carly before they got married. No, it was more because
he had high hopes for my twin Luke to take over.

So when I discovered Tori had been called by the Le
Roux, I wasn't sure who to tell. I don't want to reveal that
I'm a werebear before she's ready to know, and I sure
don't want to tell Tori she's part shifter and freak her out.

Since I finally decided to let my stepsister, Carly, train me as a tattoo artist, I figure she's my best bet. I push open the door to Ink It, where she works, and Sierra glances up from a laptop. Her eyes are big in her face, and they're accentuated by her super-short jet-black bangs cut in a straight line.

"Hey. I'm glad you're here. I have a proposition for you."

Uh-oh. Sierra has triplet boys, and I'm afraid she wants me to help. "I'd make a terrible babysitter." My coat peels away from my sweater and crackles with static electricity.

"That's not what I was going to ask. Carly and I would like to hire you to work the front desk." She holds up her hand as if I'm going to object. "It's not usually busy between clients, and it would give you plenty of time to practice. Plus we'll work around your class schedule."

I wouldn't mind hanging around the tattoo parlor, so I say, "Sounds good to me. When do I start?"

Sierra shakes her head as she grins. "Well, that was easy." The laptop clunks on the counter, and she types a bit before turning it toward me. "Just fill in the hours you can work, and I'll let you know what we can do."

The keys click as I type my name into the right slots on the calendar before me. When I'm done, I ask, "Where's Carly? I need to talk to her." I reach for my bag and lift out my sketch pad.

"She's at Kick It watching a new warrior, but she'll be back soon. Can I see what you've got?"

I glance at the notebook in my hand and realize Sierra probably thinks I want to show Carly my latest designs. "Oh. Sure." I pass it to her. Sierra's a talented tattoo artist, and I value her opinion as much as my stepsister's.

It makes me nervous to watch someone look at my work, so I ask, "Mind if I go over and find her?"

A page of my sketch pad flips, and Sierra speaks without glancing at me. "Sure. Go ahead."

I wander toward the sound of shouts and grunts. Ian notices me and smiles. He's totally hot, and my cheeks heat up a bit, because I definitely have a crush on him. Carly set me up with him as a personal trainer a while back, and I look forward to our weekly sessions. Right now he's working with the tallest woman I've ever seen. She's also a damn good fighter—she beats up a punching bag as if it were a feather pillow.

When she turns, I notice the white-blond ponytail is attached to a stunning girl. Jealousy tweaks at me, but there isn't much I can do, so I approach Carly instead.

She notices me and says, "Hey." She nods her head toward the blonde. "Pretty amazing, huh?"

I nod. "Who is she?"

"A polar bear from the Arctic." Carly turns away, and we walk toward Ink It. She says, "I've got some pig skin for you to practice on."

"Cool. I need to ask you something."

"Sure. What is it?" We've turned the corner, and the noise of the gym fades. We stop at the drink station, where Carly grabs a plastic cup.

I take a mug instead, and the ceramic handle is smooth in my fingers. "You know Tori who came in for a bear-paw tattoo?"

"Yeah. I remember her." Water splashes in Carly's cup.

"Well, she's my roommate, and that mark is because she was called, right?" I fill my mug with coffee and pour creamer in. I swirl the contents instead of dirtying a spoon to mix it.

"It is. Did she ask you about it?"

I shake my head quickly. "I haven't told her anything. But she saw the guy she dreams about the other day, and now she's kind of stalking him."

Carly gulps her mouthful of water. "How so?"

"She went to where he works and somehow got an internship. The thing is, I think he's old, like—" I almost said "like you," and Carly's smile tells me she knows it. "Well, too old for her."

"I know. She's been dreaming about my friend Keith. We're trying to find her someone more suitable."

"Oh, good."

The odor of sweat approaches us, and I glance up to see the blonde and Ian coming our way. I smile at Ian, and he says, "Lucy. Good to see you." He's a shameless flirt, but it works for me anyway when he gives me the once-over with his eyes. "You look fabulous as usual."

"Thanks." I've gotten bold with him over time, so I banter back. "You look—*hot*."

He chuckles as he reaches for a cup to get water.

"Have you met Isabelle yet?"

Ian's about Carly's age, and I know he doesn't think of me as dating material, but I haven't given up hope. I eye the girl and paste on a smile. "Hi."

She frowns at me when Ian says, "This is Lucy Robichaux."

"Are you related to Luke?"

"I am. He's my twin."

Her grin is huge when she says, "I know him."

I'll bet you do. My brother's a player, and I guess they've hooked up. But it makes me happy, because that means she's probably not after Ian. "I hope that's a good thing."

"It is." She takes a sip of water and swallows. "It most definitely is."

"Will I see you at his party Friday night?" My brother is on the board of his fraternity. It's a werebear frat, and they're known to get wild.

Isabelle frowns as she says, "No. I wasn't invited."

"Oh, it's not something you need to be invited to. It's at the Delta house."

"Delta house?"

Ian says, "That's a frat house at Orono."

Realization dawns on Isabelle's face. But she doesn't look happy, and I wonder if she has a thing against frat boys. She shrugs. "Maybe."

Ian says, "Break time's over. Let's get back at it."

Isabelle's cup crunches in her hand before she tosses it in the garbage, and I have a feeling she's got plans for my brother. But they may not be pretty.

As they walk away, I say, "Maybe I should bring Tori to that party. There will be lots of eligible werebear, and she might find one she likes."

Carly nods. "That's not a bad idea. Because Keith isn't a good match for her, and it would be nice if we could divert that attraction."

"I'll see what I can do."

Carly places her hand on my shoulder. "Thank you, Lucy. I appreciate your help."

Her gratitude makes me smile, and I'm surprised by it. When I first learned that Carly was my stepsister I wasn't pleased. But now that she's welcomed me into her life with open arms, I don't mind having a sister after all.

CHAPTER 22

Isabelle

WONDERFUL. I'VE FALLEN for a college boy. Icy wind whips around my sweaty skin, cooling me off from my workout as I pound down the sidewalk to the truck I drive. Fortunately my intense workout calmed me. I wonder if Luke's legally able to drink. Although he did get more than one bottle of wine at the restaurant for our date. But that could have been because it was a werebear hangout, and we do tend to follow our own set of rules. The familiar rush of heat to my skin as sexual desire runs through my veins is clouding my judgment, because I'd like to ignore age and be with Luke again. That man-child sure knows what he's doing when it comes to pleasing a woman. What are a few years, anyway?

I've fought the urge to call him for a couple days, because I don't do that. Men chase me. And that's how I like it. A growl forms in my throat, and the plastic of my phone case is slippery in my fingers when I pull it from my back pocket. I do need to chat with my contact about what's going on with my brother, right? I send a simple text.

We need to talk.

Luke reads it right away, and his text is quick to follow. *Busy tonight?*

Where and when? I've reached my vehicle, and a quick double beep sounds as I unlock it.

My place whenever you can get here.

An hour later, after I'm showered and fed, I arrive at Luke's. His apartment is too upscale for a typical college student, and it makes sense I didn't know he was one. The building has a doorman that needs to announce me, and I pace the small lobby while I wait for Luke to come down. The carpet is red and plush. Two leather couches are set across from each other, and a gas fireplace is burning. When we came here the other night, I must have been too drunk to remember this. Funny, I'm not a small girl and can definitely hold my liquor. That was some strong wine.

I decided to be a bit more subtle about my intentions tonight, and I wore tight leather pants with a loose top that only reveals my cleavage with its low neckline. The scent of Luke reaches me before he does, and I smile, because he's freshly bathed, too.

He bounces down the last steps and comes toward me. He's in a wrinkled Oxford shirt that has more than one button undone, and the curl of hair that has escaped makes me want to twirl it around my finger.

"Isabelle." The low rumble of his voice practically caresses my skin. Man alive, I've got to get ahold of myself.

"Luke."

"Come." He takes my arm and leads me up a short flight of stairs to an elevator. "You look lovely."

My heels click on the hard surface when we enter. "Thank you. You like nice, too." The door closes with a soft whoosh, and I notice only one button that says PH. I frown, because I don't remember this. Something about a freight elevator comes to mind, along with what we did in it. I smile with the memory.

Luke notices and turns me to face him. His hands slide up my arms. "I bet I can guess what you're thinking."

I grip his hips lightly. "Really. What?"

He leans down to my neck and places a kiss just below my earlobe. I suck in air and tip my head back in response as he whispers, "There's something about elevators that turns me on. How about you?"

"Depends on who's with me."

Luke hooks a finger in the front of my shirt and peeks down it. "Black lace. Nice."

I reach for his waistband and pull it away from his body to look down. "Nothing. Even better."

The elevator dings, and Luke steps away from me to take my hands as he backs into his apartment. I follow. Our gazes are locked, and he slips an arm around my waist to yank me against his chest. He asks, "Can we talk later?"

I place a hand on the back of Luke's head as he leans in to kiss me. *I'm all alone.* His lips are smooth and plump as he nibbles at me gently, but I'm too impatient, and I take out my hunger on him to get my point across. That added to my working on the waistband of his jeans sends the message, and he starts on my clothes, too.

When Luke begins to flutter kisses down my chest, I push him away and grab his cock. "Let's get to the good part." Shoving his chest, I back him up to the couch, and he bounces on it when he lands. I straddle his lap to get what I want. I ride him fast as I take what I need.

When I growl out my release, a sudden urge to taste his blood overcomes me. I'm not thinking clearly, because I don't realize I've done more than imagine it when a metallic flavor coats my tongue. *Shit!* I bit him.

Luke's orgasm is suddenly multiplied, and he shatters beneath me with such force that his eyes roll back in his head. As he comes back to earth, he pants out, "That was fucking amazing."

I lap at his shoulder where my bear teeth pierced him to seal the wound. "I'm so sorry. I don't know what came over me."

Luke grins up at me in his post-bite attraction. When a bear has sex and bites their partner, it forms a bond. If they aren't true mates, it's temporary, but for up to a few months, the attraction feels as if it's meant to be. Handy if you want to stay with someone who isn't your true mate, although it's frowned upon if you both don't agree to it.

And while polar bears don't punish for it, I wouldn't be surprised if the Northeast Kingdom has stricter rules.

I climb off of him and say, "I shouldn't have done that." I turn away from him and take in my surroundings as I look for a bathroom to clean up. The room is done in neutral shades with colorful paintings on the walls as artwork. My toes sink into carpet so thick that my first thought is what it would be like to lie on it.

Warm hands land on my hips as Luke grabs me from behind. "It's okay. I almost bit you the other night."

His cock twitches against my butt. I turn to him and break our physical contact. "No, it's not. I'd be pissed if you did it to me." I don't usually care about rules, but the fear of what might happen if I get thrown out of Maine is causing me to panic. "Please forgive me."

I stare at the werebear who I just blood bonded, and he tilts his head a bit as he smiles. "You're forgiven. Besides, this means I don't have to ask if you want to date a younger man." He steps close to me, and his breath is on my neck as he leans in to kiss it. "I've got my answer."

Stepping back I say, "Yeah. About that. You should have told me you're still in college. How old are you, anyway?"

"Almost twenty-one."

I knew it. He's not even drinking age. My breasts are plumped up when I cross my arms under them. "You know I'm pushing thirty, right?"

"Twenty-eight. I checked." He steps closer to trace the outline of my nipple. It hardens under his touch as tiny hairs stand up along my body. He says, "Women reach their sexual prime in their thirties, while guys tend to hit it around nineteen." The fingers of his other hand trail down my belly to between my legs. "I think we're a match made in heaven."

He slips a digit into me, and I quiver as lust surges in my body. This guy definitely has good hands. Pain shoots through me as he digs his other fingers into my bottom and yanks me against his erection. He says, "I can last all night. You?"

I whimper, and he sinks his teeth into my shoulder. The bite is sharp at first, and I cry out because of it, but it's quickly followed by heat that races through my veins as his essence merges with mine to seal our bond further. I scream with my release as he gives me the pleasure I gave him.

CHAPTER 23

Isabelle

I ROLL OVER, and the sheets under me slip. *Ugh.* Someone needs to tell Luke that satin sheets are for porn
movies and not real life. My hair sticks to my face with
static electricity from the material, and I sit up in annoyance. I pull it back into a ponytail and swipe it through
my hands to tame the flyaway strands. Tristan's been in
my head asking where I am, but I'm ignoring him. He
can suffer a bit now that I'm on my own.

I glance over at the naked man next to me. He's
kicked off the covers, and they're tangled in his feet. He's
asleep on his stomach, displaying a round, hard rump
that tempts me to take a bite out of one of the sumptuous
globes. I snort at that thought, because I need to keep my
teeth to myself.

I climb out of bed to use the bathroom. My muscles
cramp in rebellion from my workout yesterday, and that's
not all that's sore. Luke was right about that nineteen-
year-old sex drive and his ability to last all night. No
wonder he's sound asleep. When I'm done in the bath-

room, I wander to the kitchen in search of coffee. I pray the opulence of his living quarters extends to the pantry.

"Thank goodness." I spy a one-cup coffee maker on the counter, and after opening two cabinets, I find the cartridges. The cover of the machine clicks as I shut it and push the on button. While it hums, I reach for the fridge door handle and check inside. Things are looking up, because I find plenty of eggs, cheese, and sausage.

Pans rattle in the cupboard as I remove two large skillets, and when I clunk them down on the cooktop, Luke speaks, startling me. "A naked woman in my kitchen cooking must mean I'm in heaven."

I glance over at him, and damn it, he makes me smile. The goofy I'm-so-in-love kind I'm sure looks like Annie's for my brother. "Scrambled eggs with cheese and sausage."

"How about toast, too? I'll make it."

Luke is not naked, but that's probably a good thing. The sight of his chest is enough to get my blood pumping. After he drops bread into the toaster, he comes to stand behind me. I lean back into him as he slides his hands under my breasts to cup them. He says, "This has to be my favorite position. Your luscious ass cradling my dick before I bend you over and—" He lets out a low growl that reverberates through my body as if I'm purring.

I arch back and contemplate how to save breakfast. My voice is raspy when I say, "Let me plate up the food, and then let's go see how strong your table is."

The toaster pops as my spatula scrapes up eggs. Luke retrieves the bread and follows me to the dining room, where he lays me out like a meal. By the time we get to the eggs, they're cold. I swallow a bite as Tristan communicates with me in an alpha tone I have to answer. *"Where the hell are you?"*

I sigh. *"At Luke's. I'm busy, but I'll be home later."*

"Is something wrong?" Luke asks.

"Tristan and Annie are true mates."

A piece of sausage falls to Luke's plate with a soft thud. "What?"

"He bit her. I think we can safely say he's not to be trusted with the plan. Apparently it's just me now." My hand shakes as I lift another bite of food.

Cutlery clatters when Luke sets it down. He reaches for my hand. "No. It's not just you. You've got me."

I gaze into his blue eyes, so like his sister Carly's. Luke plans to betray her, and now that my brother is tied to a Le Roux, I suppose I'll betray family, too. "So what do we do?"

"We change our strategy. Let your brother believe we're still on track with the original plan."

I shake my head. "That's going to be hard. He knows me too well."

"Not if you don't have any idea what the alternative will be." He lifts my hand and threads his fingers through mine. "I've got it covered."

Trusting someone with my life isn't easy. I've got too much history that tells me otherwise. "No. I need to know what we're going to do. And I need a few days to get over the shock of my brother and Annie. I'll be fine." I pull my hand back, but he doesn't release it.

"I won't have Tristan ruining things." Luke's glare is stern.

"You have no idea who you're dealing with. I won't be kept in the dark. I've got a lot more to lose than you do. Tell me what we're doing or I'm out."

Luke turns my hand over and pulls it toward his mouth. "If you lose, so do I." He kisses my palm, and the anger that was building in me crumbles. "We're in this together, Izzy."

Luke's use of Tristan's nickname for me is nice, and I let the warmth of his lips soothe me. We may be mated by a blood bond, but I'll take it. Because with Luke, I'm not alone. Looking into his eyes, I see the kind of love I long for. The kind of love that comes from being mates. Luke strokes my cheek and traces the faint scar that extends along it. He speaks softly. "How did you get this?"

"Fight with Tristan."

He grins at me. "Must have been some fight."

"Yeah. It's a twin thing."

"I think it must be a polar bear thing." He combs my hair with his fingers. "My twin and I never fought physically."

"Lucy? I just met her at Kick It."

Luke's eyes widen. "Did you?"

"Yes. And she asked if I was going to your party. At a frat house, right?"

I move a lock of his hair back from his forehead as he says, "Uh-huh. Want to come?"

While I realize the party will be all be young college kids, I never went to a university, and the novelty of keg stands and rampant sex in upstairs bedrooms appeals to me. "I think I might enjoy that. Do you have a room where we can be naughty?"

He grins. "No. But I bet we can borrow one."

"Will there be a wet T-shirt contest?" I thrust out my chest. "Because I bet I could win."

"No. Is that what they do at Arctic U?" Luke chuckles and fondles my breast. "You would definitely win." He pinches my nipple lightly. "Naked suits you."

"It is my preferred state, but Annie frowns on that."

"If you lived here, you'd never have to put on clothes." Luke leans down and swipes his tongue over my pebbled peak.

The action sends an electric pulse to my core. *Is he asking me to move in?* I blink quickly. "That would be nice."

"Then consider it. Because our bond is going to make it difficult for us to be apart." He pulls my head toward him and brushes his lips over mine. "And because I want nothing more than to have you in my bed every night."

I kiss him back and pull away to say, "On one condition."

What's that?

"Cotton sheets. I can't do that fake stuff." I shudder a little.

Luke slides his hand between my thighs, and I open them a bit to allow better access as he says, "Anything for my natural girl. Anything at all."

CHAPTER 24

Annie

I SABELLE DIDN'T COME home last night, and Tristan is so mad that he might blaze a trail of his own. While she's brought guys home often, she's never slept elsewhere. He's tried contacting her telepathically, but she won't answer. I'm beginning to worry something happened. He stares out the window in the kitchen, and I place my hand lightly on his arm. "Would you like us to send out scouts to search for her?"

Tristan glances at me. "No. I commanded an answer, and she said slept over at some guy's place."

"Ah. Do you think she did it because of us?"

He nods. "I know she feels like I abandoned her." Tristan thumbs my lower lip as he leans down. "Izzy doesn't like you being my number one."

I could easily get lost in our kiss, but I stop him because of my worry for his sister. I pull away. "Then we need to find a way to let her know she's still important to you. What can I do to help?"

He slides his hands down my arms, making me quiver with desire. "Annie, love, you are so kind. But I don't even know where to begin. When Izzy gets mad—well, you've seen it. I'm not sure there's a way to win her back."

"Of course there is. She's hurt and lashing out, but the bottom line is she doesn't want to lose you. I think she needs you to stroke her bruised ego."

Tristan glares at me and opens his mouth, but he closes it again and turns away from me to walk toward the pantry. I wait for him to mull over what I said. Bags rustle as he calls out, "You haven't been baking. Where's the good stuff when I need it?"

"One pie coming up." I open the refrigerator to get apples and butter.

Tristan emerges from the pantry with a box of crackers. "I don't do relationships and people well. But you do."

The bag of fruit thumps on the counter when I set it down. "I'm a nurturer. I can't help it."

He sets down the box and pulls a knife out of the block it's kept in. "You're wise. The spirits know I need you in my life."

I toss him an apple, and his large hand wraps completely around it when he catches it. I say, "I wonder what they think I need from you."

He winks at me as he begins to peel the apple. "My charm?"

I snort. "Your charm almost drove me away."

Tristan's eyes twinkle as he takes a bite of apple skin. "Then it must be my body." He chews slowly and steps closer. "I give you carnal pleasure to reward you for all the good you do."

I place my hand on his crotch and squeeze. "Really now. Because I think that goes both ways."

A low noise rumbles in his chest. "Then I better start doing some good to deserve it."

I step away from him to get my rolling pin. "Begin with Isabelle."

"Fine. What should I do?"

"Anything that makes her feel special. Maybe you could take her to our land and show her where the house will be." Flour scratches at my palms as I rub it on my cutting board surface to prepare it for the pie dough.

"If she ever decides to come back."

I smile at him, because I know he heard the truck pulling up the drive. "Be nice. She's feeling vulnerable."

"Okay, but you might want to make two pies."

I send him a warning glare when the front door clicks open. He opens his mouth to show me he's biting his tongue, and I shake my head at him as Isabelle enters the kitchen.

Tristan walks over and pulls her into a hug she resists. Her arms are straight at her sides when he says, "I was worried about you."

When he releases her, she says, "Right," and steps away.

I ask, "Are you hungry? I could make you some breakfast when I finish here."

"No. Thanks. I had something at Luke's." She glances

over at Tristan to see his reaction. When he keeps a blank face, she turns to me. She grabs an apple skin and inspects it. "You know Luke Robichaux, don't you?"

"I do. He's a nice guy." Dough is soft under my fingers as I press it over the apples and onto the edge of a pie plate.

"Do you think he's too young for me?"

Isabelle is trying hard to get a rise out of Tristan, but he's doing a good job of staying in control. I answer, "Age is relative. He strikes me as a rather mature man for a college student. If he makes you happy, I don't think it matters."

She turns to her brother. "What do you think?"

"I think if you like him, then you shouldn't worry about it."

"Good." Isabelle lifts her hair up and asks, "Annie, do you have a hair tie?" She tilts her head, and a pink scar from a bite stands out on her porcelain skin. My stomach clenches in fear of Tristan's reaction.

He blinks, and a low growl comes from his throat. I speak quickly, but my words aren't heard. "Sure, in the junk drawer."

Tristan speaks through clenched teeth. "What have you done, Izzy?"

She drags her fingers down her neck and over the scar just below it. "Oh, this?" She smirks. "Love bite. You know how that goes."

My mate's hands clench by his sides, and he speaks in a slow, deliberate tone. "You bonded with Luke?"

She giggles like a schoolgirl. "Yup. And he asked me to move in with him. Isn't that awesome?"

Tristan's claws are poking out, and he's dangerously close to shifting, so I speak in his head hoping to avoid a blow-up. *"Just smile and congratulate her. She's trying to make you mad. You can do this."*

He takes a deep breath. "I hope you didn't say yes. I— I'd miss you."

I'm holding my breath as I wait for her reaction.

Isabelle shrugs. "I haven't decided." She glances at the clock over the stove. "Oh dear. I have to be at Kick It soon." She walks out of the kitchen and waves her fingers at us. "See you later."

I let out my breath and touch Tristan's arm. *"Are you okay?"*

"No."

"She was testing you."

"I know."

Tristan walks over to me, and I wrap my arms around his waist. Isabelle is upstairs, and water rushes as the shower runs. "You handled it well. Just think. She's preparing you for teenagers."

He sighs. "I'm lucky you'll be around for that."

I meet his gaze. "When do you plan to bring the rest of the clan here?"

"Once we get some housing built. I suppose my mother and kids can come once ours is done."

I reach up and stroke his jaw line. I imagine his children have the same strong features. "I'm looking forward to it. I think you were sent to me so I could finally get the children I've always wanted."

Tristan lifts my chin. "Careful what you wish for, Annie. You haven't met them yet."

"They're children. How could they be bad?"

My mate's chest quivers as he chuckles. "Annie, my love, just wait and see."

CHAPTER 25

Lucy

W HEN MY BROTHER and I were little, we were best friends. That happens often with werebear twins. But when Luke became obsessed with becoming an alpha, our relationship became strained. Even though he never exhibited the traits at puberty, he took on the characteristics and acted as if he could tell me what to do. He also befriended the Veilleux's next alpha, Victor, and they nurtured a strange alpha brother thing. But Victor was older, and Luke got into the bad-boy circuit at an early age.

Now Carly is here, and everyone knows she is the next Robichaux alpha. When Victor died, Luke had no choice but to accept that he's just a regular werebear, and he laid low. Or so I thought. Because right now I'm embarrassed to be related to him.

Tori and I are at the Delta January freeze party. And as soon as we walked in, we heard the chants: "Chug, chug, chug!" We followed the voices to find Luke and Isabelle in the center of the crowd. Phones are videoing the two of them as they each drink from a hole in the bottom of a beer can. That's one classy chick he's dating. I turn away in disgust.

Tori says, "Luke's girlfriend's hot."

"Yeah. I guess. C'mon, let's get a drink."

My purpose for being here is to find Tori a werebear our age that can distract her from Keith. I scan the room and stop when I notice Jax, a Veilleux. He's got dark hair and blue eyes like Tori's current crush, and he's a total flirt. Just what we need.

Tori is pumping the tap as I tilt a cup underneath the spout and squeeze beer out. I say, "We're going to need three. There's someone I want you to meet."

When we're done, I lead her over to a group of lacrosse players. It's hot inside, and the odor of musk and aftershave is only slightly stronger than the stale beer that has our feet sticking to the floor. The guys we approach are tall, fast, and strong. And super hot. "Hey guys, this is my roommate, Tori." She lifts a hand, and they all check her out. Being werebear, they like their women with meat on their bones, and Tori makes more than one squirm as if they can imagine holding on to a few of her attributes.

I notice Jax's beer is low, and I grab Tori's arm to whisper in her ear. "Offer the extra beer to the guy with the electric-blue eyes." I speak loudly, "Hey, Jax. Tori plays left forward, too."

His male ego is pumped, and he steps over as if he's clearing the crowd away to let them know she's his. I elbow Tori, and she says, "Um, I have an extra beer. Do you want it?"

Jax flashes her his million-dollar smile and wraps his hand around the cup, making sure he overlaps her fingers. He holds her for a moment as he tries to hypnotize her with his gaze. "Thank you." She blushes, and he tilts his head. "I love this song. Wanna dance?"

My inner cheerleader shouts "Yes!" as he leads her away. I check out Jax's friends and notice Dillon. He's dark blond and has a smoldering look that works for me in so many ways. He offers me his signature smile that only turns up half of his mouth. "Lucy, Lucy, Lucy, setting up the friend and leaving yourself out in the cold. C'mere and let me warm you up."

I shake my head. "And just how many girls have you used that line on tonight?"

His friend Eric speaks up. "You're the first."

Dillon punches his arm without breaking our gaze. "Freshmen."

I grin back at him and hold out my hand. "Dance?"

Winding our way through the crowd, I lead him to where Tori is. She sees us and stops to take a big swig of her drink as she waves at me. Dillon and I dance next to them, and the four of us last until our beers are gone. Tori is the first to wave at us to get more to drink.

She shouts to me as we make our way to the keg. "Jax is great."

I nod. "You should go for it."

She wiggles her eyebrows at me. "Maybe I will."

As we get closer to the beer, cheers get loud, and I

groan when I see why. Isabelle is standing on her hands. They're braced on top of the keg, and the spout is in her mouth. Luke is watching with a sappy look on his face as if she's the greatest thing he's ever seen. What is wrong with him? Then a realization hits me like a two-by-four. Is Isabelle his true mate?

Fabulous. I could be linked to the blond nightmare for life. I move toward Luke, but I don't manage to get near enough before Isabelle hops down and throws herself into his arms. She lets out a belch, and they both laugh.

Ewww. I shake my head and turn away. The geeky freshman Eric is by my side. "Hey, want to dance?"

Since Dillon is nowhere in sight, and Tori went back to Jax, I say, "Sure."

I take us close to where my roommate is so I can spy on her. The music is so loud that the floor shakes with the bass. Jax is making his moves, and when he pulls her against his chest and kisses her neck, she throws her head back to enjoy the sensation. Mission accomplished.

I yell so Eric can hear me. "I have to go to the bathroom. Catch you later, okay?"

He nods at me, and I exit the dance floor to go stand in line. Fortunately there's only one girl in front of me, and I lean back against the wall to wait. Tired and ready to leave, I let my eyes close for a moment. But my peace is short lived.

"Lucy."

I snap my eyes open to Isabelle. I sigh. "Hi."

She grins at me and lifts her hair up off her neck. Her fingers trail down and flutter over a pink scar. *A bite mark*. In the werebear world, it's like showing off a diamond ring you want someone to notice. I'm tempted to ignore her actions.

She says, "Frat parties are fun. I've never been to one before."

I nod. "Seems you're making the best of it."

"For sure. I want to try everything I've ever heard about."

I wonder what B-rated movies she's seen that inspired her recent actions. "I'm sure you'll get to come to more."

She giggles, and the sound makes me want to vomit. "I know. Especially since Luke and I are mated."

I refrain from rolling my eyes. "I thought that was a recent bite. Good for you." Sincerity is lacking in my voice, but it's so loud I doubt Isabelle can tell.

"Thanks. I guess that means we'll be seeing a lot of each other."

The door to the bathroom squeaks open, and I'm saved. "Guess so." I hurry in to put a barrier between us. As I relieve myself, I try to find the good in this situation and decide at least she'll make it easier to hide from my parents' scrutiny at family functions, because I'll bet they're going to be all about Isabelle. I'll get to be the golden child. The thought makes me smile.

CHAPTER 26

Tori

T HE FLOOR OF the frat house is vibrating with the sheer volume of noise, and the music playing travels through my limbs as I dance with Jax. The T-shirt he's wearing is tight, showing off a muscular body that begs to be touched. And I'm touching it, because he pulled me in close, and we're bumping against each other as we move and hold our beers away from ourselves in an attempt to keep them from spilling. I can't help that his chest keeps me from falling when someone bumps into me, right? The way his abs flex under my fingers makes me linger, and his smile tells me he doesn't mind.

It might be the alcohol, but something about this guy reminds me of Keith, and I find the scent of Jax strangely attractive in the same way. The fact he keeps sliding his hand over my butt helps. He likes my fluffy body, even if it's only for tonight. When he leans down to kiss my neck, I throw my head back and let him.

My uptight Connecticut prep school was full of rail-thin girls that got all the boys, while my two sisters and I were left out. I don't know how Ginny and Nessa are doing at Bowdoin, but here at UMO, there's a whole lot of guys that like their women curvy, and I'm getting male attention I've never had before. I had no idea college would be this great.

Lucy is dancing next to us, and when I've drained my beer, I decide I want more. I wave at her and then yell at Jax. "I'm going to the keg!"

He points toward the bathrooms. "I'll catch up to you!"

I nod at him, and Lucy leads the way through the crowd. I gush a bit over the Jax, but I stop when my friend freezes. Isabelle is doing a handstand on top of the keg and sucking on the pump. Gross. We're supposed to pour beer out of that when she's done?

I glance at Lucy and see she's horrified, but I bet it's about a lot more than germs. I would be too if that were my brother. She's making her way over to him, and I want no part of the drama. I grab one of the pitchers full of beer being passed around and pretend Isabelle was the first person to suck out of the tap as I refill my cup.

I wander back to the dance floor and search for Jax. He catches my eye and smiles as he makes his way through the crowd toward me. Oh yeah, frat parties are fun. When he gets to me, he leans in close and asks, "Want to go cool off outside for a bit?"

I nod and let him take my hand to tug me along. Icy air greets us as when we step outside, and I relish the feeling on my overheated skin. I move to the porch railing and lean against it. Lukewarm beer fills my mouth when I take a sip. Jax seems to have lost his cup, so I hold mine out for him to drink from it.

"Thanks." He swallows slowly before he asks, "Freshman, right?"

"How did you know?" Lucy is a junior, and she got me as a roommate this year because it's my first year in the dorm, too.

"You have that wide-eyed look of wonder as if this is your first frat party."

I open my mouth to protest but realize he's teasing me. I snap it shut to grin instead. "I've been to a couple. They're not usually my thing."

"How so?"

"They're so—I don't know. Animalistic."

Jax snorts out the sip of beer he took. "What makes you say that?"

I shrug. "That's not the right word. I'm not sure why I said it. I guess what I mean is nobody seems to have a filter at these. It's as if they're acting on pure instinct, and the need for pleasure isn't restrained."

Jax hands me the beer. "Whoa, what the hell am I doing out here. I'm going back inside." He moves like he's leaving me and stops to chuckle.

"You're such a tease."

He waggles his eyebrows at me. "I hope that's a good thing."

"It is." I drop my gaze as my face heats up.

"Hey." Jax places his hands on my hips, and I glance

up into his sparkling blue eyes. "Don't be embarrassed. I like you, too."

"You do?"

He nods and leans down as if he's going to kiss me.

Oh my god! My body lights up as I wait for his lips to meet mine. I don't dare to close my eyes in case I'm wrong. His touch is light as if he's testing me, and I part my lips slightly to nip at his bottom lip. Jax nips back and pulls away.

"Are you playing lax this spring?" he asks.

"Um-hmm." My ability to speak words is temporarily paralyzed, and I take another sip of beer to hide it.

Jax smiles as if he knows I'm flustered. "Indoor training starts next week. But I've already started lifting at the gym. Want to work out with me this week?"

"Sure. But I have to warn you, I'm in terrible shape right now."

He gives me the once-over with his gaze. "Doesn't look that way to me."

I try to hide my blush as I wrap my arms around myself. The cold is finally making me chilled. I speak quickly. "Where and when?"

"Monday at three." He takes the beer from my hand and sets it on the railing. The movement brings him closer to me, and his chest rubs against mine, making my nipples harden at the contact. I think he feels it, because his voice gets a little deeper in tone. "I'll be the guy at the squat station."

My voice is breathy when I say, "Okay." Jax places his

palms on my upper arms and rubs to warm me up. His hands are hot, and I flash to the memory of Keith's touch. My voice returns to normal as I say, "Sounds good."

This time when Jax kisses me, his tongue enters my mouth, and I close my eyes to get lost in the sensations. I place my hand on his chest and press against his defined pecs. Pecs that make the image of Keith pop into my head again. I squeeze my eyes shut more as if I can send the vision away, because fantasizing about the older man while I'm kissing a hot guy more my age is so wrong. I focus on kissing Jax back.

His hands cup my butt, and he pulls me against his groin. A large erection between us is an invitation to go further. I pull away and break our kiss to gently decline. "I should go find Lucy. She was pissed at Luke, and she'll probably want to leave soon."

"Sure. I'll see you Monday?"

"Yes." I step backward toward the door. "Squat rack. Three. I'll be there."

"Good. I look forward to it, Tori."

I wave before I enter the humid frat house. It doesn't take me long to find Lucy. She sighs in relief when she sees me. "I was looking for you to let you know I'm leaving."

"Everything okay?" I ask.

"Yeah. But I've had enough. Where's Jax?"

"I left him on the porch. I'm ready to go, too."

Lucy walks toward the kitchen, where we stashed our coats in an empty cabinet. There's a side door, and she says, "Let's go out this way and avoid the crowd."

A spoiled-fish odor wafts toward us from the dumpster, and it makes me crinkle my nose as Lucy asks, "The sexy Jax didn't convince you to hook up tonight?"

"Nope. But we're working out together Monday." The frat house isn't far from our dorm, and I pull my jacket closed, while Lucy doesn't. That girl has an internal heater that rivals those of most guys I know.

"Good. He's not a player, if that's what you're worried about."

"Yeah, I didn't get that vibe. He was super nice," I say.

"And he's our age."

I chuckle as I recall Lucy referring to Keith as a senior citizen when I told her how old he is. "There's that, too." Honestly, though, his age doesn't dissuade me one bit. If anything, it makes him sexier. Maybe I should have let Jax take me up to a room and help me forget the man I can't have.

We've reached our dorm, and I pull my key out of my coat pocket. The metal ring it's on is cold in my fingers. I swipe the plastic card through the reader and pull the door open. While I'm tired, I'm a little afraid to sleep. Because I know I need to find a way to let Keith go, and having him star in lurid sex dreams doesn't help my resolve. I sigh.

"What's the matter?" Lucy asks.

"I'm hungry. Want to order a pizza?"

"Sure. I'm not ready for sleep yet either."

"Luke and Isabelle?"

"Yup."

"Maybe we should order ice cream, too? And then you can tell me all about it."

She grins at me. "Sounds like a plan."

CHAPTER 27

Annie

W HEN TRUE MATES find each other and bond, they spend a few weeks thinking about nothing more than how to connect physically. But it does begin to fade over time. Tristan and I have been together for a month now, and our pillow talk about the little things has evolved into creating memories as well as sharing stories about ourselves.

I glance over at the man I love sitting at the kitchen table. His strong fingers wrap around a coffee mug, and he lifts it to take a drink as he reads something on his tablet. I take my cup and a plate of homemade donuts over to sit across from him. He turns his attention to me. He smiles as he lifts a pastry, and bits of sugar fall down like a light snowfall. "Is this to make me feel better?"

I offer a sheepish look. Isabelle finally took Luke up on his offer to live with him, and she left yesterday. "Does it?"

He reaches over and takes my hand. "Everything you do helps. Thank you."

Tristan feels it is his job to take care of Isabelle, almost as if he's her father instead of her twin. Having her rely on another man is a tough loss for him. "I have a surprise for you today. Have you ever been snowshoeing?"

My mate chuckles. "Whatever for?"

It does sound silly when as bear we are so much faster in the snow, but something about trudging along as a human with a backpack picnic is romantic to me, so I say, "It's a lot easier to carry our lunch that way. I thought we'd hike to the spot where our house will be built."

I get the smile I was hoping for. "That's a lovely idea. We do have something important to talk about." He sighs. "I fear bringing my children here is going to ruin what we have."

The way Tristan talks about his kids, you'd think they were spawns of the devil. "Nothing of the sort will happen."

"If they don't, then it will be my mother." He shakes his head.

I want to get moving, so I say, "You can tell me all about it later. Now go get changed for a trek in the snow. I've already packed our picnic."

When we're ready to leave, Tristan is in a playful mood that makes me glad I came up with this idea. He's attached his snowshoes, and I laugh as he begins to plow through the snow. He shuffles for a bit and stops to turn back to me. "Am I supposed to march? Or just walk normally?"

"Try to walk normally. Watch me." I move in front of him, and snow lifts up from the backs of my snowshoes to hit me in the butt.

Tristan chuckles. "Oh, I like this view so much better."

"Of course you do. Maybe I'll show you what we can do with the blanket I packed."

"Dessert after lunch. How decadent."

I look back at him over my shoulder. "Who said I'd wait until after lunch?" I begin to jog, and my mate catches up to me quickly and catches me by my shoulders so I'll turn to him.

"You know, I could shift, and you could ride on my back. It would be so much faster."

"We've barely gotten out of the yard, and you're tired already?"

"Nope. I'm thinking about that blanket and don't want to wait."

"Hmmm." He makes a tempting offer. Tristan brings out my carefree side, and I've become less rigid in my thinking, so I throw my hands up in the air. "Fine. Give me the pack and shift so you can carry me."

"Thank god." Tristan leans down to take off a snowshoe. "These things are awful."

I watch shamelessly as he strips off his clothes. When he's almost naked, I lick my lips and gaze at his spectacular body. "You're right, this is a much better idea."

He winks at me. "Five minutes and I'll be saying the same thing." He folds his clothes neatly, taking extra care with his pants. He places them in the backpack and then stands to shift. My mate is magnificent, and the process that takes his large Adonis-like male form and transitions it into a polar bear is amazing.

When he's done, I take a moment to marvel at his sheer size and beauty. I say, "You have to be the sexiest creature I know."

I slip the backpack over my shoulders as Tristan lowers himself to the ground in a crouch for me to climb on. I remove my mittens and stick them into my jacket so I can grip his fur. It's slick in my fingers with his natural oils, but I manage to secure myself on his back. "Ready."

He begins to walk with me, and I think he's making sure I'm stable. I say, "Run. I want to feel what it's like as a human."

When Tristan takes off, I hang on for all I'm worth. The air whipping around me as his powerful muscles flex under me is thrilling. We arrive in less than five minutes, and my fingers are cold when he lies on the ground for me to slide off. When he shifts back, he says, "One sexy creature at your service."

"Then my command is you kiss me."

Even though he's naked in the cold temperatures of February, he still manages to burn like a furnace as he pulls me against his body. When I've become a quaking mess, he stops kissing me and asks, "How was your ride?"

"Amazing. I think you're damn hot as a bear." I slide my hand down between us and grab onto his hard cock. "But as a man…" I let out a growl and stroke him. "I find you irresistible."

Tristan peels the backpack off my shoulders and fumbles with the zipper. "Where's that damn blanket?"

I let go of him as I laugh.

He gives me a mock glare and asks, "And why aren't you getting naked?"

I grin and scramble to accommodate him. "Oh, sorry." I let my clothes fall in a heap and step close to Tristan, who has the blanket over his shoulders. He wraps it around me, and we sink down in our embrace.

WHEN THE CHILL in the air is too cold for me to stand it any longer, I lift myself off Tristan to get dressed. He lies on the blanket and watches. "You are such a beautiful creature, my love. I don't think I'll ever tire of looking at you."

He's sprawled out as if it's a mid-summer day. "You don't get cold, do you?"

"No." He sits up and grabs his shirt from the pile of clothes I set out for him. "I don't think I'm going to like your summer."

"Probably not. We'll have to install air conditioning and keep it set at fifty." I yank my snow pants up over my long underwear, and the closure snaps shut.

"Ah, that would be wonderful."

When we're dressed, I begin to pull out our lunch. I discover champagne. The bottle is moist in my hand, and I pull it out. "Did you put this in here?"

"I did." Tristan takes it from me and starts the process of opening it.

"What a nice surprise." I set the glasses down on the blanket and begin to lay out the food.

He says "Stop. First we need a toast."

"Okay." I pick up the plastic cups so he can fill them.

When he's done, Tristan shoves the bottle into the snow so it's standing upright and rises up on his knees to dig in his pocket. He pulls something out but keeps it in his hand. My heart beats faster as I imagine what it might be, and I give him his glass. He says, "Put your hand out."

I hold it out palm side up, and he places his fist on my hand to open it and trap an item between us. It's small and hard and has a sharp edge that digs into my skin. My heart flutters with excitement when I guess it's a ring. Tristan says, "I often think it would be nice to be human for this. The element of surprise is gone when you meet your true mate."

I shake my head. "I'm surprised, Tristan. Don't ruin it for me."

He grins. "Annie Le Roux, will you marry me?"

I can't help it. Tears roll down my face, and I nod. My mate removes his hand, and I glance down at my engagement ring. I gasp, because the diamond I assumed was a long, skinny marquis is actually a huge emerald-cut stone. "Tristan."

He takes the ring, and I flip my hand over for him to slip it on. The stone is the size of a piece of gum, and the setting has fine cutouts in an elegant filigree design. I twist my finger to catch the light. "It's gorgeous."

"It was my grandmother's, and I know it's old fashioned, but I hope you like it."

"I love it." I throw my arms around him and spill champagne down his back as I lose the grip on my glass and it tumbles into the snow. "And I love you." I kiss him. I'm not sure what happens to his cup, because both his hands are on me as we do our best imitation of fusing together as one.

Tristan takes my face in his hands, and they sear my cheeks as he whispers, "Forever, Annie, my love. I'll love you forever."

"I'll love you forever too, Tristan."

CHAPTER 28

Isabelle

I RESISTED MOVING in with Luke because I know our bond isn't forever. But after a couple weeks of watching my brother with his true mate, I couldn't take it any longer. My love affair with Luke may be manufactured by biting each other, but it's all I've got.

The large flat-screen TV is on, with some woman interviewing celebrities and making people laugh. I have a dozen magazines in front of me, and the pages are slippery in my fingers as I flip through one. I find it annoying that nothing seems to capture my interest. The publication slaps down on the pile when I throw it, and I stand up to pace over to the thermostat.

My hair is stuck to the back of my neck, and I lift it up as I check the temperature. It's sixty, and even though I'm naked, I can't seem to cool off. I've probably had four cups of coffee. Other than my daily workout at the gym in the afternoons, I've got nothing to do.

I wander into the kitchen, where the tile is cool under my feet. Leaning against the stainless steel refrigerator door, I sink to the floor to sit and yawn as I stretch out my legs to have more contact with cold things. I stare at my painted toenails and notice a chip. Maybe I'll give myself a pedicure.

The familiar noise of the elevator sounds in the distance. Well, at least I know what I'm doing for the next hour. I bet my mate has come home between classes for sex, but even that doesn't appeal to me today. I don't move to greet him and wait as the door snicks open and his footsteps thump lightly on the carpet. I detect his arousal, and it should turn me on. God, I'm in a pissy mood, because suddenly our relationship feels cheap.

"Isabelle?"

I mumble. "In here."

Luke comes around the counter and tilts his head at me. "What are you doing?"

"Nothing. Absolutely nothing."

"Uh-oh. Is my girl bored?" He raises his eyebrows. "I can fix that."

The idea that I'm here for sex whenever he wants it niggles at me, and I decide to turn the tables. "Strip."

Luke begins to take his clothes off, and I bark out. "Stop. Give me some Magic Mike. Let me see the sexy swagger that drives women wild." My mate thinks he's the best lover I've ever had and brags about how women can't get enough of him. I've done nothing to let him think otherwise, but the truth is every guy I've been with believes that.

I hold back my laugh as he swings his shirt over his

head and lets it fly across the room. I smile and say, "Give me some hip action."

Now we're talking. Luke begins to move and drags his hands down his chest. He turns as he lowers his pants so I get a view of his round butt. I growl a little to encourage him. When my mate turns back around and straddles my legs in a standing position, his cock is at my face, and I know what he wants, but I raise my hand and say, "Back up and start at my feet. Seduce me."

He frowns but does as I ask. *That's right, buddy.* I smile as he gets on his hands and knees and kisses my foot. *Today it's all about me.* By the time Luke's mouth gets to my thighs, I'm warming up. I spread my legs and slouch down against the fridge to enjoy my mate's talented tongue. Luke doesn't disappoint, and my mood improves greatly after my first orgasm.

Luke doesn't stop there, though, and I wonder why he's not taking what he wants when he lifts me up to the kitchen counter and begins to give me a repeat performance. I lean back on my elbows and gaze at the man between my legs. He's working me over as if I'm all that matters. I thread my fingers through his hair, and he lifts up to shove his fingers inside me. "Izzy, what is it?"

My eyes flutter shut as he hooks his finger and massages my g-spot. "I don't know. Things just feel wrong today."

"Let me chase the blues away." Luke continues to work me with his hand as he lowers his mouth to suck, too.

Oh god. I scream with my climax this time. My mate is relentless, and he doesn't ease up with the sweet torture of his tongue. He is making it all about me. I revel in the attention and let him bring me up again.

I lose count of my orgasms and am a puddle of quivering muscles when he finally stops. I'm sprawled out on the granite countertop, and Luke asks, "Can I carry you to the bedroom? I'm not even close to done yet."

I lift my head up. "What?"

"I haven't been taking care of you, Isabelle. I'm so sorry." He scoops me up in his arms and begins to walk. The scent of me is on him, and my bear growls with pride. Luke whispers, "Let me make it up to you."

An hour later, I'm sleepy as I cuddle into my mate. He plays with a strand of my hair and asks, "What can I do to make you happy?"

"Nothing. I'm just in a mood today." I sit up when I realize how long he's been home. "Wait. Don't you have class?"

"I'm skipping it. You're more important."

"I am?"

"Yes." He lifts up to kiss my thigh above my knee. "It's my job to take care of you. So I'll ask again." His mouth moves up higher on my leg. "What is it that you need to be happy?"

I open my thighs as he moves to the inside of them. I can't believe I'm wet again considering he's got to have broken any orgasm record I had. "Something to do."

Now his breath is hot on my sensitive slit, and I begin

to tremble. "What interests you?" He asks.

He sucks my clit in, and I arch up. "I don't know."

Luke lifts his head to hover over me as he thrusts fingers inside me. "Then we'll just have to find out."

I nod as I fall back on the bed and let my thoughts be all about pleasure.

I RETURN FROM the bathroom after a quick shower to find Luke is missing. The sheets are a tangled mess, and the room reeks of sex. My body is deliciously sore as the wood of a drawer scrapes when I open it. I'm due at the gym in a half hour, and I pull on workout clothes.

When I'm dressed, I go to the kitchen for a snack and find Luke dumping fruit in the blender. He smiles at me. "One protein smoothie coming up."

I'm reminded of the sweet things Tristan would do for me when I was having a bad day. *Luke cares about me.* The whirl of the blender sounds, and when it's done I say, "Thank you."

"I have something else that might cheer you up."

I take the drink from him and swallow down a creamy mouthful. "What's that?"

"You need something to do, and the Robichaux warriors need to step it up. How would you feel about being the assistant trainer?"

"But I train with the Le Roux." I slide onto a stool and glance over the counter at him.

Luke leans on the surface toward me. "Exactly. Your

job is to make sure whatever they do we do better."

The plan. I grin at him over my glass. "I like it."

Luke reaches for my hand and holds it tight. "I love you, Isabelle. Together we'll both get what we want. We've got a wonderful future ahead of us."

"I love you, too, Luke." I imagine a life with him and picture a wedding and small blond children. I smile at my mate.

He cups my cheek with his hand. "I'm your family now, Izzy. I'll take care of you. Promise."

Warmth spreads through me at his words. *He really does love me.*

"What are you saying?"

"I had this whole thing planned where I was going to take you to the restaurant where we first met. But I can't wait."

I recall the way he fingered me to an orgasm under the dinner table before we'd even ordered. "Patience isn't our strong suit, so don't."

"Marry me."

I lean over the counter. "Yes." I grab the back of his head and kiss him. While our kiss usually turns into so much more, I hold on to the simple connection this time, because it's a symbol of love. The kind of love I crave.

When we break apart, Luke says, "You make me so happy."

Tears burn in my eyes, and I whisper, "You want me forever."

His teeth gleam in the daylight. "Yes, Izzy, I do."

PART 3

CHAPTER 29

Annie

TRISTAN HOLDS A cut-crystal glass of clear liquid up to the daylight shining into the kitchen of our new home. He swirls it and watches as if something unusual might happen. I wait for him to speak his mind. He lifts the drink to his nose and says, "Did you know that besides the sting of alcohol, humans find vodka nearly odorless?"

My mate inhales the scent of the cup's contents and closes his eyes as he savors it. "They love to speak about the bouquet of a fine wine. The undertones, the over-tones, the body." He holds the glass out to me. I lean down to sniff it as he continues, and my nose burns. "But vodka? They can't detect a thing." He lets out a growl. "They'll never fully appreciate this."

Tristan has brought his family business to Maine by reinventing it. While his history as a distiller is the De Rozier clan making illegal moonshine in a shed, he's taken his knowledge and created a trendy handcrafted vodka brand.

Arctic Ice Vodka will debut in a few weeks. Between the new business and building our house, I've been so busy that I can hardly believe it's late spring. The glass thumps on the table when I set it down. I say, "It doesn't matter. They don't know what they're missing. And it certainly won't stop them from buying."

My true mate's dislike for humans was a surprise. He grew up interacting with very few, while the Northeast Kingdom werebears led normal human lives in the public eye, paying taxes, going to the public schools, and being treated as equals. The Northeast Kingdom is so integrated into the human population that many werebear even get romantically involved with them before choosing a mate.

But Tristan believes humans are the reason he no longer has his kingdom and has to rebuild a life for his clan here in Maine. His prejudice is understandable, but I hope one day he'll see how good humans can be.

Tristan comes over to stand behind me and wraps his arms around my waist. I lean back against his chest and bask in the heat of him as I gaze out at our land. Freshly cut garden beds of dark, rich earth glisten with frost in the early-morning sunlight. I'm looking forward to planting my favorite perennials next month.

Tristan is unusually quiet this morning, and I ask, "What's wrong, love?"

He gives me a squeeze before relaxing his arms and grabs the cup on the table. "Nothing." The odor of alcohol wafts toward me as he dumps the contents of the glass into the sink, and it splashes on the stainless steel.

When he turns to me, a smile covers his face. "I'm off to the distillery. What's your plan for today?"

My mate has done a one-eighty with his mood, and I wonder about his morning ritual of pouring himself a drink he never takes. It started with the first batch of vodka, and at first, I thought he was monitoring the process. But now that his recipe has been perfected, I question the reason. I say, "The landscapers are coming, and I've got the painters starting on the upstairs bedrooms." I glance at the clock on the stove. "They'll be here any minute."

Tristan places a quick kiss on my lips. "Well, then we'd better start our workday."

I grab his shirt. The starched cotton is stiff between my fingers. "Wait." I'm not sure what's churning in my mate's head, but I need to break through his icy exterior. I tug him close and kiss him with passion. He seems startled but warms up quickly.

When I pull away, he growls, "Thanks. I needed that."

I reach up and place my palm on his freshly shaven face. "Think you can push the papers off your desk for—" I pause and waggle my eyebrows at him. "Lunch?"

He nips at my neck with his bear teeth. "You know I will."

"Good."

I watch him leave, and I am happy I could make him smile. But my worries set in. Once Arctic Ice Vodka makes its rounds with the critics, it will need to be put into production. That means hiring workers, and the plan is they'll be from the De Rozier clan, who have yet to arrive. While I would love to provide homes for the families, we can't afford to buy eight houses for them. We opted to build a dorm-like structure for the clan members to use for free until they've accumulated enough savings to venture out on their own. Tristan assures me that it will be luxurious compared to their current accommodations.

Plates clash as I open the dishwasher to put Tristan's glass in. He hides his past well. My mate's appearance is one of wealth, even though his family riches are long gone. But it's not only the accommodations I'm worried about. I wonder how the clan is going to assimilate into a world that isn't familiar. If Tristan is prejudiced against humans, I suspect his clan is, too.

A dull ache forms behind my eyes as I ponder what I signed up for being next in line as the De Rozier prima. I've got hellion children, an evil mother-in-law, and numerous bigoted polar bears coming soon.

I force myself to think of happier thoughts, like our wedding. I wanted to do it here, but Carly insisted we have it at her house so she could take care of the details for me. A quick glance out the window at the dirt pile that is my lawn makes me glad I agreed. I make my way down the hall to the front door to greet the painters clamoring on the porch and shake my head that I was so distracted I didn't hear them pull in.

Once I've let them in to do their work, I pull out my sketches for the gardens. The paper rustles as I spread them out on my kitchen table. I want to mimic the gardens at Brady's house, which I designed and cared for. Only instead of a fountain as the focal point, I think a pool for Tristan's children would be nice. I'm sure they're full of energy, and swimming year-round should help exhaust some of it.

The roar of a motorcycle catches my attention, and I smile to myself. Gabriel's on his way, and even though the temperature is still frigid outside, he's on his bike because the roads are clear. I grab the teakettle, and the gas stove flickers when I turn it on. I pull out the Earl Grey tea he favors and a container of honey.

Movement outside catches my attention, and I discover Gabriel is taking stock of what's been done to the yard. I go outside through the back door and call to him, "I know you're going to make this mud pit look amazing, right?"

"Of course I am." His blue eyes sparkle as he loosens the ponytail he must have worn for his ride. His hair is shoulder length and dark blond, like that of many of the Le Roux.

"Come on in, and let's take a look at my plans. I'm hoping you'll give it your magic to make it sing."

Gabriel removes his shoes at the door, and his sock feet thump softly as he walks to the table. He pores over my drawings as I prepare his tea. Water splashes into the large mug, and Tristan's voice sounds in my head. *"I hope I'm not interrupting you, darling."*

"Never. What is it?"

"I just got word my mother is on her way, and I want you to be prepared."

"Should I practice my self-defense moves?"

My mate chuckles before he answers, "Perhaps. But you only have two days."

"Two days? Your mother will be here in two days?"

"Yes." Tristan sighs. "Our honeymoon may be over before we start it. Please remember why you love me, because she has a way of poisoning all that's good about me."

"Tristan. I don't believe it." But my stomach clenches, because I don't want to share my mate with a woman he hates.

I glance over at Gabriel, and he asks, "Everything okay?"

I nod. "It will be. But when we're done here, let's take a walk. I need you to help me decide where my future mother-in-law should live."

The vision of a chain-link fence topped with swirled barbed wire flashes in my mind. Unfortunately, I don't think that would be the best way to welcome Tristan's mother, so I tuck the image away and put on a brave smile as I hand Gabriel his tea and prepare to listen to his plans for my lovely gardens.

CHAPTER 30

Tori

MY PHONE BUZZES with a text. I glance down to see it's from Jax. I've been trying to like him for weeks now. I open it but don't reply to his attempt at seeing me tonight. Lame, I know, and unfortunately, the more I put him off, the more he wants to see me. I wish I could find a way to make Jax be the guy I want, but I still can't shake my dreams about Keith—or my impure thoughts the moment I walk into Bear Mountain Lumber.

The scent of fresh-cut pine overpowers the musky smell of spring when I step out of my car. My internship is one day a week, and I spend the other six waiting for it to come. The parking lot is almost empty, and it makes me wonder if maybe I'm not supposed to be here. My phone is slick in my hand as I double-check my calendar to see if I missed a text from Keith telling me my day is cancelled. When I find nothing, I pick my way through the mud puddles toward the door.

I'm assigned to a different area of the manufacturing

plant each time, and the location is dependent upon who has the time to show me what they do. I go to Keith's office to check in. His door is always open, and I find him digging through a pile of papers on his desk when I get there.

"Hey."

He glances up and smiles. Heat rushes all the way down to my toes as he says, "Hey. I'll be right with you."

"Where is everyone?"

"It's shutdown day," Keith mumbles and then slides a document over as he says, "Got it." He returns his gaze to me, and his eyes twinkle. "We're going to do routine maintenance on the machines. It's pretty fun, because sometimes we have to fix things."

I smile at his boyish excitement. "Oh, yeah?"

"C'mon. Pierre is waiting for us."

My work attire is jeans, multiple layers on top, and steel-toed boots. Our feet clunk down the hall, and we stop to get our hard hats and ear protection before entering the manufacturing section of the building.

An older man in a flannel shirt with the sleeves rolled up over a tight T-shirt comes our way. Even though he's got gray hair, the guy is cut, and muscles ripple in his arms as he lifts a toolbox. I've met him once, and he's a man of few words, so I nod back when he acknowledges me with a tip of his head.

Keith raises his eyebrows at me when Pierre just keeps walking, expecting us to follow. I cover my mouth to suppress a giggle. The old guy must have eyes in the back of his head, because he grabs a container of oil and tosses it over his shoulder without turning around or stopping. The oil slaps into Keith's hand as he reaches out to catch it. Pierre says, "Driveshaft."

Keith mouths to me, "Driveshaft."

I mouth back, "Stop," as a grin covers my face.

My relationship with Keith is easy. He openly teases me as he shows me things and treats me like I'm a little sister. It helps me contain my physical urges even though my crush on him continues to grow. Throughout the day, we proceed to grease and clean the heavy machinery, and I even get to replace a big part on one of the saws. To say I'm in heaven is an understatement.

When it's midafternoon, we break for milk and cookies. Cold, creamy liquid slides down my throat as Keith says, "Told you today would be fun. I saw you do a little happy dance when we got that saw running again."

"It was. My mother and sisters would have rolled their eyes at me."

I watch Keith's throat work as he swallows a bite of his cookie before he says, "Yeah, but your dad would have been proud."

I shrug. "I wouldn't know. He was never a part of my life."

"Oh. Sorry for the faux pas."

"Don't be. It never really bothered me." I get up to refill my glass, because I'm lying. Growing up without a father was a big deal to me for a few years. I wasn't into the girly things the way my sisters were, and I wished I could have spent my weekend days hanging out in a garage, tinkering.

My glass chills my fingers as I return to the table, and I say, "My mother managed to parent just fine, and the one time I complained about no man in the house, she pointed out to me there were no guarantees my father would have even been the mechanical type." I let out a small chuckle. "And then she taught me how to do the physical-labor chores she hated. I filled my need to fix things by changing out the storm doors for screens and cleaning out the gutters." I break off a piece of my cookie. "It was a win-win."

"Did you ever get to work on a car?"

"No." I tilt my head at him. "Don't tell me you have some old sports car you restore."

"I prefer landscaping." He frowns slightly before he adds, "I spend my weekends turning my yard into a mystical forest."

A piece of my dream comes back to me. Keith and I are in a wooded area that makes me think of a children's story version of wilderness. "Mystical? Like a fairy—" Heat rises to my cheeks, because what we do there is X-rated.

When Keith lifts his gaze to me, his eyes are dark, and he swallows as if his cookie is stuck in his throat. He reaches for his milk. The glass topples, and he picks it up quickly. Dabbing at the small puddle with his napkin, he mumbles, "We should get back to Pierre."

I wonder what I said to upset him as I clear my

things. On our way out of the cafeteria, he walks quickly, and I catch up to him to grab his arm. "Keith. I'm sorry."

He stops and turns to me. His jaw is working, and he rakes his hand through his hair as he sighs. "You have nothing to be sorry for. I'm the one who should apologize."

"For what?"

"For making sure I spend time with you whenever you're here."

"But you don't." My stomach sinks, because I'm afraid he'll stop being around when I come in. His mouth is a tight line, and I don't think I'm getting anywhere, so I yank out my phone. "I know we can never be together. Let me show you something. Look. I have a boyfriend." The glass is smooth under my finger as I tap in my password. I pull up my texts and show him the one from Jax. "See?"

Keith glances at the screen and then back at me. Now his eyes are hard in a different way. I'm not sure my lie made anything better, because the heat radiating from him almost sears me. "Is it serious?"

"Ah. Yes?" I sigh. I'm a terrible liar, and my lips give me away when they part as if to ask for his kiss. "No. But the point is I'm not waiting for you. I know we'll never be a thing."

"He treats you right?"

Now I'm confused. He's being protective? I step back to put space between us. "Sure. I mean—yes."

"Okay. Let's go look at the kiln controller." I follow

Keith as we walk toward the back door. As soon as we're outside and on our way to the building where the wood cures, he's back to his usual self and stomps through a puddle to get me wet. I return the favor, and we end up laughing as our pant legs get soaked during a childish game. But the one we're playing isn't for kids.

CHAPTER 31

Isabelle

I'VE HAD A lot of crap jobs in my lifetime, so doing data entry at Kick It is a breeze because it means I'm clean, dry, and able to drink as much coffee as I'd like. But mostly, I'm happy to have something to do besides work out. I shut down the membership spreadsheet, and the computer snaps shut when I close it. As I stand, I grab my empty mug to wash it out. I have a session with Ashton in fifteen minutes.

I decide to catch up with Luke. *"Hey, Babe, sushi tonight?"*

Cohabiting when you're mated takes away the angst of wanting to be together, but it doesn't rid couples of the power struggle that can happen when first sharing living space. Luke and I came to the decision that we would alternate cooking dinner. I don't usually do takeout, but I do pick easy meals to make. Slicing up fish and making a salad falls into that category.

"Sure. I'll be home by seven."

Luke likes to get his studying done before he comes

home. His discipline is admirable, and he's managed to get enough credits in his three years that he'll graduate this spring with a degree in business. I'm trying to convince Tristan to hire him for Arctic Vodka while Luke studies for the test he needs to apply to law school, but my brother is still bitter that we mated.

When I walk over to the drink station, I notice Lucy working the front desk at Ink It. I call out, "Hi, Lucy."

She glances over at me and offers me her fake smile. I pour on the sugar. "You really must come for dinner some night. I know Luke misses you."

Now she snarls in reply, and it makes me grin. I enjoy nothing more than getting under the skin of werebears who don't like me. I turn away and notice Ashton has arrived, and I walk over to the mats where we'll start.

That first day Ash and I worked together, I sort of lost it on a punching bag. I haven't pulverized one since, because he pulls me back before I get there. It shouldn't work, because only Tristan, who's an alpha, can stop me. But when Ash tells me to stop, I can.

He gives me his usual silent nod, and we begin with a jump rope routine. My muscles are tight but begin to loosen, and our ropes become a blur as I try to keep up with his speed and footwork. My heart pumps and pushes oxygen through my limbs as I fall into the zone. When I begin to reach exhaustion, Tristan interrupts my trance.

"Izzy, Mom is coming. Tomorrow."

I freeze in place as my body goes cold. I reply. *"Please don't make me see her."*

The slap of Ash's jump rope stops, too, as Tristan says, *"You have to. But I won't leave you alone with her. I promise."*

My stomach clenches, and I place my hand on my belly as if I can make it stop. Sweat drips down my nose and splatters on the floor. *"Right. And you promised to not bite Annie. We know how that worked out."*

Tristan's voice is faint. *"She can't hurt you anymore, Izzy."*

"I know." I bend over and blink back the tears that burn in my eyes. My mother may be too old and frail to hurt me physically now, but if her voice still works, she'll find a way to do it with words.

Ashton asks, "Are you okay?"

I glance up at him. "Yeah. I'm fine." I hop up to bounce on my feet. "My brother was just telling me my mother will be here soon."

Ashton steps back and crosses his arms. "Punching bag."

He's cut the jumping drill short, but I don't mind. The familiar burn of anger rolls in my veins as I begin the level-one progression I use to warm up my arms. My punches are hard today, and the scent of the adrenaline racing through me is so strong that I can smell it. I think Ash can, too, because he moves me on to level two quickly. My feet smack at the bag, and the chain it hangs from squeaks as my force moves it.

"Three!" Ash's voice rings in my ears, and I begin more-complex moves. The pain I crave comes as the impact of my punches spikes into my bones. *Yes.* When I deliver a roundhouse kick, the slap of my foot is followed by a ripping sound, because I break through the leather of the punching bag. It's as if I've opened up the well of evil I keep locked inside me, and my movements become faster while my hits become so forceful that the agony reaches my spine.

I'm lost to my rage, and I let it pour out of me as I destroy the object before me. When there's nothing left to hit, I stop and step back to hunch over and catch my breath. I'm suddenly aware that Ash is in front of me, and I glance up at him. He tilts his head toward a separate room used for yoga classes.

When we get there, he sits down and motions for me to do the same. "Tell me about her."

Tears run down my face as if a dam has broken, and I begin to speak. I tell him about the abuse I suffered as a child from both my parents. I talk about how everyone in the clan knew and nobody stepped in to help the alpha's children. I talk about why I learned to fight and tell him about the first time I struck back and how I spent a week in a cage as punishment. And when I'm done, Ash holds me as I cry out the tears of a lifetime.

Once I recover, Ashton finally speaks. "Why don't you let your bear out when you're here?"

Intense anger makes it hard to control shifting. I gaze into his blue eyes and notice the high cheekbones in his face. His jaw is strong, and his neck is as thick as a tree trunk. I don't think I could kill him, but I'm not sure. I say, "Because she's afraid."

He nods at me, and I wonder about what he must have seen in the human wars as a SEAL. I whisper, "You know, don't you?"

Ashton shakes his head. "I only know what you tell me, Isabelle." He hands me a towel. "Maybe someday, you will."

The cotton is rough against my face as I wipe away sweat and tears. I offer a wry smile and jump up to my feet. "We've got time for a sparring match. You up for it?"

Ashton gives me his version of a grin. "Bring it."

CHAPTER 32

Annie

I'M ON THE Internet searching guest cottage layouts when Tristan gets home. I'm so engrossed that I don't get up, and when his hands land on my shoulders, I jump. He leans down and kisses my neck. I say, "Do you like the looks of this?" I tilt the screen of my laptop so he can view images of a beach-house-inspired kitchen.

"Vacation home?"

"No. I was thinking your mother might like it."

When I met Tristan for lunch this morning, I didn't mention my plan to research building his mother a house of her own. I wanted time to think about the idea. Now I hope it's a good decision.

He says, "She's staying here." Tristan walks over to the freezer and pulls a bottle of vodka out. The stopper pops when he yanks it out, and a glass clinks on the counter.

"She doesn't have to." I turn in my chair to face him. "I can afford to build another house for her, and then we can have our privacy."

Tristan takes a sip of his drink and closes his eyes. I'm not sure if he's trying to find words or if he's had a rough afternoon. When he opens them, he stares at me for a moment before he says, "My mother does not like to be on her own. She stays here."

From what he's told me about the elder Mrs. De Rozier, I don't think she's going to like me, and I don't relish the idea that I'll be living in my home with a woman who makes me uncomfortable. But Tristan seems firm on his stance, so I say, "Fine."

I do tolerance well, and I bet Tristan will want her gone before I do. I say, "The Lupine Room will be ready for her. Do you know what time she'll arrive?"

"I'm picking her up in Portland tomorrow afternoon. We'll be home for dinner."

"What should I cook?"

Tristan sighs and holds the chilled glass up to his forehead. "I don't want to talk about her. Can we discuss it tomorrow?"

"Sure." I walk over to him and wrap my arms around his waist to lay my head on his chest. His shoulders relax as he slips an arm around me and pulls me tight. He downs the glass of vodka, and I imagine the burn in his throat. I speak telepathically. *"You can tell me anything."*

"Did I mention the children are coming, too?"

"What?" I pull away and glare at him. "I'm not ready." I put my hand on my forehead as I start to pace. "We need beds, and their room isn't painted, and—" Panic makes my pulse quicken, and I stop to look at

Tristan. "Why didn't you tell me?"

"They're just kids. They don't need special things."

I frown before it hits me. He and Isabelle were always an afterthought, so why would he think his children should be any different? I walk back to my mate. "Oh, Tristan." His face has the beginnings of stubble, and his cheek is rough against my palm when I place it on his cheek. "I'm going to shower them with love and give them the childhood you should have had."

Tristan's eyes glisten, and his hand is warm over mine as he pulls it from his face. "Annie, my love, I don't deserve you."

"Of course you do. Don't you realize the gift you're giving me? Children, Tristan—the very thing I thought I would never have."

His lips turn up the slightest. "You don't get it. My kids are no gift." He holds up his hand as I open my mouth to speak. "Tell me what you think in a week, but for now, don't be grateful, because our love is about to be tested by my family."

I grin at him. "You forget I've met Hurricane Isabelle."

He allows me a small chuckle. "She'll seem like a gentle rain after you meet the rest of them." He pulls me back into an embrace. "Let's have dinner on the porch and enjoy the stars." He gazes down at me. "It will be the calm before the storm." He kisses me, and I taste the rich flavors of spice in his vodka before they give way to the familiar sensations of my true mate.

WHILE I SEASON the steaks, Tristan opens a bottle of red to let it breathe. I'd be concerned about his drinking, but he went for a run after his earlier cocktail, and I'm glad he chose exercise to relieve his tension. I smile as I think about the other workout we had when he returned. While he continues to warn me about his feral offspring, I can't help my excitement. I'm about to have three five-year-olds giving my home the activity of a family.

The meat slaps on the platter, and I say, "You haven't told me if you have boys or girls, and I want to know their names."

My mate's mood is positive, and he says, "Girls. Eva, Echo, and Ellie."

"Goodness. I was expecting boys with harsh Nordic names that make me spit when I say them."

Tristan's eyes twinkle. "You mean like Satan and Lucifer?"

"Exactly." I hand him the steaks and a large spatula. "You have no idea how much fun I'm going to have with little girls."

Tristan kisses the top of my head. "If anyone can tame them, it's you, my love."

While he steps out to the back porch to grill, I rinse off the fiddleheads I picked up from a roadside stand. I'm going to sauté them in lemon butter, and I nibble on one as I walk over to the fridge to get the ingredients.

I fantasize about the summer days full of trips to the lake, going out for ice cream, and learning to ride bicycles. Maybe we can install a playground for all the children in the De Rozier clan. Butter sizzles in the pan, and I turn down the heat as I squeeze in lemon juice. Even though I'm anxious to get things ready for the girls, I know Tristan needs tonight to be all about us.

When he comes inside, I grab the bottle of wine and hand it to him. "Let's toast to finding each other. Because you continue to make me happier every day."

Wine gurgles into the oversized goblets as Tristan pours, and I toss the greens into my sauce before I take my drink. He says, "To finding the woman who makes me fall in love all over again each day."

"To finding the man who makes my dreams come true." Our glasses clink, and the acidic taste of vinegar accosts my senses when I take a sip. I turn to the sink to spit it out at the same time Tristan does, and the contents of our mouths splatter. "Ugh."

"It's gone bad," says my mate.

"Let me go get another bottle." I grimace as I roll my tongue around my mouth to clear the unpleasant taste, and I jog down the stairs. The air in the basement is cool, and I entertain the thought of making a playroom down here for the polar bear children who are sure to find our summer too hot.

When I return, I say, "Let's try this again." I notice the empty bottle on the counter. "You poured it out?"

"Yes. There's nothing you can do with it once it's turned."

I nod, because I would have done the same thing, eventually. Although I probably would have entertained another way to use it first. "I suppose you're right."

CHAPTER 33

Annie

B REAKFAST AT THE house that used to be my home is strange. Especially when I come in to help cook, and things have been moved around. Utensils rattle in a drawer as I search for the tongs I like to use for bacon.

Carly hands them to me. "Here. Sorry, I haven't been very good at keeping things up to your standards."

I wave my hand at her as I move over to the pan that pops with sizzling pork. "It's your kitchen now."

"Maybe so, but you had it organized with precision, and I'm ruining all your systems." She bumps my hips with hers. "And we really miss your cooking. I don't like not having you here."

"I miss you, too." I turn to her so I can see her reaction. "Guess what's arriving at my house this afternoon?"

The waffle maker beeps, and I remove golden-brown squares to place them on a plate. I grin at Carly. "Tristan's mother and three five-year-old girls."

My sister-in-law squeals. "Triplet girls? Oh my gosh, Annie, you're going to have so much fun."

"I know. I can't wait. Only I'm going to have to scramble to get things ready for this afternoon, because Tristan only told me last night."

"How strange." Carly's spatula scrapes against the pan as she loads a bowl with eggs. "Why the secrecy?"

I shrug. "I'm not sure. But I think it might have to do with his past. Either that, or he was trying to ignore it."

"Huh?" She hands me a plate for the bacon. "Well, in any case, let me know what I can do."

Mother breezes into the kitchen like a gust of wind. "Triplet girls. Goodness, Annie, you're going to have your hands full."

Carly laces her words with a hint of sarcasm, "Good morning, Donna. Was that your way of offering to help?"

I chuckle, because I have every intention of employing my mother.

"I adore children. You know that." Mother places the teakettle on a burner, and the gas starter ticks as she turns it on. "Just let me know when I should come by."

I say, "I'm not sure what we'll need to do for care when they get here, but I suspect we'll have a wardrobe shopping trip. Summer's going to be quite the culture shock."

"Oh, that's right," Carly says. "Living on a glacier must be cold year-round. I bet all the humans will be a bit overwhelming for them, too."

"Do you suppose they're feral little beasts?" Mother is joking, but maybe only a little. Isabelle's temper tantrum when she blazed a new trail in our woods left quite the impression on her.

"Stop," I say. "They're going to be lovely little girls who need a little TLC. You'll see."

Carly hugs my shoulders with an arm. "Well, you're the woman to do it. Nobody has a bigger heart than you do."

Brady has entered the kitchen, and a cabinet clicks as he opens it to get a mug. "What's this I hear about little girls? Are Tristan's kids here?"

"They're coming today."

"Wonderful. I can't wait to meet them."

Carly says, "I know what we should do. You should come here for a barbecue this weekend." She winks at me and turns to Mother. "I'm sure Donna's dying to meet your mother-in-law-to-be."

Mother snorts. "I'd rather have a root canal. I've heard she's a bitter woman."

"Mother." My tone is stern. "We don't know that."

"While I applaud your ability to always see the best in people, I'm afraid you're in for some difficult times, dear." The teapot whistles, and she removes it from the stove. "But every one of us is here to help. Just say the word."

Keith and Ashton come through the back door, and they're laughing when they enter. Mother walks in front of them to go sit with her tea and says, "Good morning, gentlemen."

They say in unison, "Donna." I grin when they try to cover whatever they found funny with boyish smiles.

Keith notices the basket of bear claws Carly made and grabs one. "I love these things." I watch the happy version of my friend and smile. While the loss of his mate, Taylor, will haunt him forever, he's making progress, and it's nice to see.

Voices are loud and cheerful as everyone loads up a plate and settles down to eat. I take a moment to reflect on how wonderful the leadership of the Le Roux clan is. Much of it is due to my mother's insistence on our weekly breakfasts to maintain our close bonds. I hope I can nurture the same thing when I become prima of the De Roziers.

Brady catches my eye and communicates with me. *"What are you thinking over there?"*

"I'm giving thanks for this and hope I can turn my new family into the same loving environment."

"Deep thoughts. But don't worry. You have a knack for this."

"Thanks."

I take my place at the table, and my astute mother asks, "Keith, rumor has it you have an adorable co-ed intern working for you. Seems she's putting a little spring in your step these days."

Keith is used to my mother's teasing and takes it in stride. "Tori's made me realize I should let the career placement office at Orono know I'll take interns. Her enthusiasm is contagious."

"Tori?" Carly asks. "Is she still dreaming about you?"

Keith shrugs and puts a forkful of food into his

mouth.

"My, my. Be careful—we don't need her heart broken," says Mother. She frowns. "I should get a bead on Delia's boys."

"Nothing's going on," Keith says. "You've got nothing to worry about. She's like a little sister to me."

"Hmpf," says Mother. "I'll bet. You're probably having the same dreams."

One of the characteristics of the call we put out was that the two to be mated would experience dreams that predicted their future, and we discovered they were often the same sexy fantasy for both participants. Keith's cheeks flush pink, and he clears his throat. "She has a boyfriend."

Mother lifts her teacup and speaks over it. "I don't suppose you know who the boyfriend is? Is it a Le Roux?"

Keith shrugs and shoves food into his mouth.

Brady takes pity on his best friend and changes the subject. "Ash, how's Isabelle's training?"

"Good. She's a gifted warrior."

"Excellent. I thought we might use her for the mission to Southern Maine. We need to rein in the rogue clan before trouble with humans breaks out. The reports I'm hearing aren't good."

Ashton taps the side of his head. "She's not ready."

I frown, wondering what he means, even though I think he's talking about her anger-management issues. I glance at Ash, and he holds my gaze as if he's trying to tell me something. I make a mental note to ask him about it later.

But first things first. I've got Le Roux business to get through and a new family to prepare for. I sip my coffee and smile with my excitement. A new chapter in my life is about to begin, and I can't wait.

CHAPTER 34

Isabelle

I PUSH MASHED potatoes around on my plate with my fork. Ever since Tristan let me know my mother's coming, I've lost my appetite. She should be here by now, and dread is a lump in my stomach as I wait for my brother to insist I see her. Luke's talking about something, but his voice is white noise. A cool hand on my arm startles me, and I glance up into his face. "What?"

"You haven't heard a word I said. What's wrong?"

"My mother's in town."

Luke doesn't know much about my past, but he does know that my father is dead and that I don't get along with my remaining parent. "Have you seen her?"

"No. But I'm sure that's temporary." My fork is loud when it crashes against the plate.

"Would you like me to go with you when you do?" Luke picks up the bit of potato I splattered on the table and sets it on the side of his plate.

He's so sweet. If only I believed he could actually protect me. "Maybe. But you're going to meet her at some point, because she's moved to Maine."

"Right. She'll be living on the land the Le Roux gave your family."

I nod and reach for my glass of wine. Suddenly, the need to get numb is strong, and I try to be discreet about drinking half the glass by taking a large mouthful. Luke has mentioned he thinks I drink too much, and I don't want his judgment.

"So where will she live? With your brother?"

"Um-hmm. And I'll be summoned when she's ready for me."

Ever since the day I broke down with Ashton, memories have been flooding my mind. I'm reliving incidents of my parents' cruelty in my nightmares Things I'd forgotten, and I haven't been getting much sleep.

My bear is unhappy, too. She's always at the surface, wanting to get out, and I've had to run every day to keep her calm. Otherwise…

I reach for my glass again and lift it to my mouth. I take another large mouthful and wonder if the tannins in the red wine stain my tongue the color of blood.

"Hey, where did you go?" Luke asks.

I shake my head. "Nowhere." I paste on a smile and reach for Luke's arm. "Tell me about your day."

He frowns. "I just did." He lifts my hand and threads his fingers through mine. "What's going on in that head of yours, Izzy? You've been distant for days now."

"It's nothing." I turn away to avoid his gaze.

"It's something." Luke grabs my chin and turns my

face back toward him. "I know you've been having nightmares. Jumping out of bed and locking yourself in the bathroom to cry doesn't hide them from me."

I pull away from his touch and grab my wine glass to empty it. "I don't need your pity."

Luke sighs. "Izzy, you're in pain, and I want to help."

I get up and grab the wine bottle. "There's nothing you can do." I fill my glass again and walk over to the couch to sit nestled in the corner. I let the overstuffed cushions cuddle me.

Luke walks toward me and lowers himself slowly on the sofa to face me. He growls, "You underestimate me. There's a lot I can do. Tell me who's causing your nightmares, and I'll take care of it."

I'm not sure what Luke means, but for a moment, I'm tempted to ask him if he can put a hit on my mother. But I shake my head, because I don't need her death on my hands. My past already haunts me. "I wish it were that easy."

"Do you want to talk to somebody? I have resources."

"You mean a shrink?" I gulp down another mouthful of alcohol. "I'll be fine."

"So you're just going to drink yourself into a stupor and pass out until your horror wakes you up again?" Luke stands up and glares at me. "Great plan."

I tilt my glass at him. "Works for me."

"Actually, Izzy, it doesn't. When you're ready to try something that will, let me know." He walks off, and silverware clashes on the dinner plates as he clears the table.

I should get up and help, considering he made dinner, and the deal is the cook doesn't have to clean. I guzzle the rest of my wine and go to the kitchen to take over.

I put my arms around Luke's waist as he rinses dishes at the sink. "I'm sorry. I don't mean to take it out on you." I kiss his neck and slide my hand down his pants. His cock twitches against my palm.

"Don't. Sex isn't going to chase your demons away."

"No?" I undo the waistband of his pants with my other hand as I grip his shaft. The skin is hot and silky in my palm. "Then maybe I'll just have to convince you of the benefits."

Luke's chest vibrates as he growls, and he turns around, quickly releasing my hold. He grabs my arms. "Seriously. Every time I try to dig below your surface, this is what you do."

I drop to my knees and yank his pants down, and his dick springs free. "Doesn't look like you mind." I suck him into my mouth before he can protest more.

"Damn it." He groans and holds my head. He tries to push me away, but I take him so far into my mouth, my lips hit the skin of his groin. Luke shudders and says, "Yeah. You're right. I don't mind."

I let out a low rumble from within as he bumps against the back of my throat. I speak to him in our heads. *"That's it, baby, push it in. Fill me up."*

Luke's grip on my scalp gets tighter as he pumps his

hips. I swallow so that my throat closes around the tip of his cock, and he says, "Jesus, Izzy, what you do to me." His body begins to quake, and his butt clenches in my hands as he gets closer. When he tries to pull out of my mouth, I don't let him. I suck harder and drink in his release.

I sit back and wipe my mouth with my arm as he sinks to the floor to face me. "God, I love you." His strong hands hold my face as he kisses me. *"One night of sexual healing, coming up."*

Luke stands as we continue to kiss, and he pulls me up. He scoops me up in his arms as he kicks his pants off his feet. When he drops me onto the bed, the springs squeak. I lean up on my elbows to watch him remove his shirt. *"You are so sexy. I want to ravish every inch of you."*

"Uh-uh. My turn." My mate crawls over me and tugs my yoga pants and thong. When he gets to my feet, he sucks in a toe and sends a shiver down my spine. He bites in teasing, but I wish it was harder.

I throw my head back and whimper for more. Still on my elbows, I arch my back, and my nipples are hard against the cotton of my T-shirt. I didn't bother putting on a bra after my shower, and I sit up to remove my shirt as Luke moves up my legs with his nipping. He's using teeth, and I moan as I fall back onto the mattress. When he gets to my inner thigh, he bites hard, and I yelp.

"Too hard?"

"No. That's what I want. Make me feel, Luke."

He growls and latches onto my sensitive slit. His

tongue thrusts as he sucks my folds. His teeth close around my clit quickly, and the pain gives way to a burning sensation that makes my juices flow. *"Don't stop."*

Luke digs his fingers into my butt, and I squirm in ecstasy at the relief I feel when he lessens his grip. *"You like this. Should I spank you?"*

"I don't know." I've never had sex mixed with pain before, but I'm definitely getting off on it.

Luke's voice is deep when he says, "On your stomach, hands over your head."

I roll over obediently and am surprised when he slaps my bottom. The sting makes me growl. And my mate rubs where he hit me. I say, "Again."

"Hold on to the headboard."

I slide my hands under the wood and grip it tightly.

He slaps the other side, and I groan. "Oh, God." I gyrate my hips as if I can create the friction I crave. "Touch me."

His fingers reach between my legs, and I squirm under his touch. He hisses in amazement, "You're dripping wet." He removes his hand, and I let out a small noise of disappointment as he commands. "On your knees. And don't you dare let go."

Now I moan and say, "Please, Luke. Please."

"Please what?"

"Hit me harder."

Luke's hands stroke my bottom as if he's trying to erase the mark. "Izzy, you're already going to have a bruise."

"Damn it. Just do it!"

He slaps me again, and I growl, *"Yes. Again."*

"I—"

"Again!"

This time, he strikes hard and swears. The burn is so sweet, but it's ruined when the mattress bounces as he gets off the bed.

"What the hell? Where are you going?"

"I can't do this. I can't hurt you like this, Izzy. It's wrong."

I roll over and notice he's no longer hard. He's not the fierce warrior I thought. He shakes his head as he stares at me. I recognize that look. *I'm not crazy. Don't leave.*

I sit up and say, "C'mere."

Luke crawls back on the bed, and I hold my arms open for him. "Come love me."

This time, my mate is tender, and while my first orgasm is good, it's not exceptional. My mind drifts away from what's happening as Luke continues to thrust into me. He rubs my clit and does all the right things to bring me another climax. My body responds, but it's as if I'm watching us from above. *I can't feel it.*

Luke pants out, "I love you, Izzy." His teeth poke out of his mouth, and he lowers himself to my neck. The moment his canines graze my skin, I flinch away.

"No."

He pulls back with confusion.

I shake my head as tears form in my eyes, and I whisper, "I mean yes." The searing heat of his bite gives way to the intense pleasure I crave, and I sink into the abyss of the mate bond.

CHAPTER 35

Tori

Last Thursday, my internship ended. Keith gave me a hard hat as a going-away gift, and we promised to stay in touch. In a weak moment a few days later, I sent him a text. I invited Keith to my final presentation, and he said yes.

I smooth out my slim-fitting skirt and tug on the bottom of my cropped jacket. "So this isn't too much for Maine?" I ask Lucy. My suit would fit in perfectly with my mother's country club crowd, and I don't want to overdo it for my professor.

"You look smart."

"Thanks." She doesn't know I'll be seeing Keith and that part of my concern is what he'll think. I'm hoping he will see me as an equal instead of as a kid.

I grab my bag and leave for class. My heels click down the hall as I remember how to walk in them. When I get outside, the warm breeze blows my hair back and tickles my neck as I run my speech over in my head.

"Tori!"

I glance to my right to find Jax jogging my way. He's dressed up, too, and he grabs his tie as it tries to swing over his shoulder with the wind. With our busy lacrosse schedules, we don't see much of each other, and I've been able to keep our dating casual.

I stop and wait for him to catch up. He says, "You look fantastic. Final presentation?"

"Yes. You, too?" I really should give this guy more of my time. He's gorgeous in his suit that must be tailored to his body.

"Naw, I wear this every day." His eyes dance as he holds out his arm. I hesitate for a second because Keith might see us, but I shake the thought quickly. "Let me escort a beautiful lady."

When I hook my arm in Jax's, I notice the pleasant scent of spicy cologne. It's faint, but since he never wears one, I comment, "You smell good."

When we get to the door, he holds it open and winks at me. "So do you."

I wish that adorable gesture made me tremble, but it barely registers on the Richter scale. I point down the hall. "I'm that way."

He releases me and says, "Upstairs. Go get 'em."

"You, too." I make my way to the classroom and enter it to find the two other presenters hovering over the projector. We were all told to come early and make sure our visual aids are in order. I sort out my things and wish them good luck.

A few minutes later, people begin to arrive, and my

nerves make my palms sweaty. I'm second in line to speak, so I take a seat in the front row. After the fourth time I swivel around to see if Keith has come, I realize how ridiculous I must look and make myself stop. It doesn't take long for me to realize I didn't need to check, because my tattoo begins to itch. When I turn again, I find Keith's gaze on me as he settles into a seat. He holds up a thumb. I return the gesture before facing front again.

The silly grin on my face would give me away if anyone looked, and my anxiety is overcome by my happiness. The first student's speech flies by even though he drones on about working in a meat processing plant, because I'm busy reliving the fun I had with Keith.

When it's my turn, I manage to get through my presentation without missing a beat. I find Keith's familiar smile encouraging as I share the highlights of my internship at Bear Mountain Lumber, and at the end, he gives me a wink that sends a bolt of lust all the way down to my toes.

Damn it. I'm not doing so well with the crush that can't be had. When class is over, I make my way to him. He shines like a beacon in the crowd with his strong presence, and I'd be drawn to him even if he were a stranger.

"You were great," he says. "Even I wanted to do an internship next semester."

I grin at him. "Thanks. But you deserve all the credit. It was fun because of you."

When we get to the hall, he steps aside to let students

pass. "I'm glad. It's not often I find someone who likes the way things work the way I do. I enjoyed having you."

This should be goodbye, but I hang on to the tiny thread left between us. "Can I buy you an ice cream?" I offer a sly smile. "You are missing milk-and-cookie time."

"Ah... sure. Lead the way."

When we get outside, the melodic song of birds chirping makes me notice the tiny spring buds are now full leaves. White flower petals are scattered on the ground.

Keith's face falls as he says, "This is bringing back memories of when I was here. Do they still have black raspberry?"

I wonder if he's wishing he were younger. "They do. Is that your favorite flavor?"

"Yes."

My shoes click up the concrete steps to the student union. "Mine, too."

He smiles, but it's not quite full. "I should have guessed it. We're an awful lot alike."

Yeah, but you still don't want me. I lead us to the counter, where a plastic window reveals the ice cream. I say, "Two large cones please, black raspberry." The paper napkins whoosh out of the container as I grab extras and hand them to Keith. I say, "If we're so alike, you're going to need these."

He chuckles, and when he takes them from me, I think he purposely avoids touching me.

Once we have our treats, we go outside, and I walk us

over to a bench. I perch on the edge, and when I cross my legs, Keith's gaze lingers on them. My skirt has hiked up high on my thighs, and I don't pull it down. I watch him lick his ice cream and wish I could taste his tongue.

He says, "You look so grown-up today."

I sigh. Obviously, I read his body language wrong, because he still sees me as a child. "I am grown up."

Keith stops eating and stares at me for a moment before he drops his gaze. "Yes. Yes you are."

I stare back and do my best impersonation of telepathic communication. *Oh Keith, please act on what we have.* While I know he didn't hear me, I could swear he moves in closer. Or maybe I do. His scent is tantalizing, and the little bit of purple ice cream on his lips makes me want to stick my tongue out and lick him. Now I'm sure I lean in closer, and I'm about to close my eyes when he flinches back and laughs as he lifts his cone to show me the drip running down his hand.

Shame burns its way up my neck when I realize he wasn't going to kiss me after all. I'm so stupid. I take a bite of my cone and crunch it as I fall back on the bench. The metal back of my seat is hard against my shoulder blades.

I gaze ahead to see if anyone watched my embarrassing move, and I notice Jax is walking toward us. I wave my arm as I stand. I say to Keith, "There's someone I want you to meet."

Jax quickens his step as he comes to us. "How did it go?" he asks.

"Great." I turn to Keith as he stands. I notice how in his dress shirt and slacks, he's the magazine-spread fantasy of women compared to Jax, who'd be more likely to grace a gossip rag for girls. I say, "This is Keith. He was my boss."

Jax sticks out his hand, and I slip my arm around his waist, as if it can erase my blunder, and say, "And this is Jax."

Keith's eyes narrow, and I swear a low rumble comes from his chest as he grabs Jax's hand. I know one comes from Jax, because the vibration hums against me. I glance back and forth between them as they hold on with a death grip longer than they should. *What the heck?*

I look up at Jax. "So how did your presentation go?"

The guys release each other, and Jax smiles at me. "Really well." He leans down, and this time, I know I'm going to get kissed. "Black raspberry, yum." Jax's lips meet mine, and I open up to it—because this is how it's supposed to happen.

When we stop, Jax says, "I've got to run. Practice is in a half hour." He turns to Keith. "Nice to meet you, man."

Keith's eyes flash with something not quite real, and a chill down my spine makes me shudder.

I say, "I've got to get moving, too. Thanks so much for coming."

"You're welcome." Keith reaches for my napkin and wads it up with his to toss it in the garbage can near the bench. "What are your plans for the summer?"

"Don't know." I pick up my bag, and the weight of

the strap is heavy on my shoulder. "After finals, I'll be looking for a job. Maybe I'll go to Boothbay Harbor and wait tables with my sisters."

"Don't. Come work for me."

I blink quickly. "Ah. Are you sure about that?" My heart hops up and down in a jig.

"Yes. If you can't stay in the dorms, I can help you find a place to live. I think you'd love Maine in the summer."

Whoa. First he won't kiss me, and then a little get-even ploy on my part makes him want me to stick around? I don't know about this.

"Thanks for the offer. I'll think about it. I really do need to go." I start to walk backward and say, "I'll text you. Thanks again."

"You're welcome."

I turn away and avoid shaking off the heat I feel from his gaze as he watches me.

CHAPTER 36

Annie

SOMETIMES I AMAZE myself. I twirl slowly around the pale-pink room that now has three single beds, three dressers, and three bookshelves waiting for little-girl things. I toss a sequin-adorned pillow on one of the beds and want to squeal. I'm about to get three little girls to raise as my own.

I didn't get this much joy out of decorating Tristan's mother's room, and at the moment, I'm ignoring the anxiety I feel about meeting her in less than an hour. The beep of the timer on the stove begins, and it's incessant, so I make my way downstairs to pull out the blueberry cake I made for the new members of my family.

Tristan sends me a telepathic message. *"Just got off the interstate. Be there soon."*

"I'm ready. Anything I should know?"

"They're tired but seem happy. Tonight should be fine."

I take a deep breath. That's good news, and I pull out plates, glasses, and the brightly colored plastic cups I purchased for the girls. I hope they like homemade lemonade, and I wonder if that's something they drink in the arctic.

The leftover heat from the cake wafts toward me when I open the oven to put the lasagna in to bake for dinner. It's my go-to meal for welcoming people to my home, and I've yet to come across someone who didn't like it.

I glance at the bottle of red I have on the counter. I never thought to ask Tristan if his mother drinks. I shake my head, remembering the wine last night that had turned and decide it might be an omen, so I grab the thin neck of the bottle and move it to the pantry. It's slimy, and I wipe it with a towel quickly. I can always pull it out if we want it later.

When I check on the guest bathroom for the third time, I finally hear the rumble of our Hummer coming up the drive. *They're here.* I step out the front door and wait on the porch. Grass is beginning to sprout, and it appears as a faint-green haze hovering over the dirt.

The car stops and ticks for a bit before Tristan opens his door. I move forward to greet my new family members. Three small girls get out in a tangle; they gain their footing, and I notice how thin they are. My nurturing side can't wait to fatten them up. A woman with hair void of any color takes Tristan's hand as she stands. She takes me in slowly, and I reach out to her. She appears to be much older than my mother, and she's not what I expected. Although while I thought her frail, her grip says otherwise when she grasps my fingers and gives me a powerful squeeze. I say, "Mrs. De Rozier. It's a pleasure to meet you."

"Call me Helga. Thank you for having us." She turns to the children. "Girls, introduce yourselves."

I smile at them as little voices tell me their names. I reply, "Welcome, Ellie, Echo, and Eva. Come on inside and have some lemonade." Their necks are craned as they stare up at our house. I turn to follow their gaze and imagine my home through their eyes. It does look a bit like a fortress with three stories and oversized doorways to accommodate the height of my fiance and his clan. Even the windows appear impenetrable with the decorative wrought-iron grates.

As we walk up the steps, I turn and ask, "Do you like blueberries?" I get nods and wonder if they're shy. "Good. Because after dinner, I have blueberry cake for dessert." And I plan to whip some fresh cream to get more calories into the wee things.

I imagine the kids are hungry, and I offer them a snack as they settle in to play with coloring books and their dolls in the great room. Tristan, Helga, and I retreat to the kitchen. I ask Helga, "Have you ever been this far south?" A plastic tray is slick in my hands as I pull it out for the girls' food.

"No. This is the first time I've travelled a great distance from my home. The scenery is wonderful."

"I suppose getting used to all these trees will take a while."

Tristan says, "I think you'll like it, Mom. There's so much to look at, and I know how you'll be fascinated by the detail."

He says to me, "My mother's a painter. She does lovely watercolors."

The older woman smiles. "You're kind. They're nothing special. Just something I do for fun." Her glass scrapes on the wood table as she twirls it around, and I watch and wonder why she's fidgeting. She notices and asks, "Is there anything I can do to help for dinner? I'm terribly antsy."

Tristan scowls at her, and I say, "Sure. I could use help with the salad."

"I'll take you for a run after dinner, Mom," says Tristan. His tone is cool as if he's scolding her.

The cutting board thuds on the counter, and I hand her cucumbers and a knife. Helga says, "Yes. I think I'll need that, too. Thank you."

I glance at Tristan to see if he wants to explain what's going on, but he avoids my gaze, so I bring peanut butter crackers to the children. When I return, I stare in amazement at Helga chopping the vegetables as if she's in a race. But when she starts to hum and move to the beat of her song, her happiness is contagious, and I join in and grab a tomato to dice. I'm not sure what Tristan meant by his mother being difficult, because right now she's very pleasant.

Dinner is a delight. The girls are polite but answer my questions when asked. Helga makes us laugh with her funny stories, and I wonder if the death of her difficult husband has allowed sunshine back into her life. I'm pleasantly surprised that this is not the woman I expected from Tristan's veiled warnings. I smile with relief that she's going to be a positive addition to my family.

After dinner, Tristan takes his mother out into the woods, and I run a bath for the girls in my oversized tub. I let them each have a special scrub puff and pour in lavender bath salts so they'll feel pampered. When I lift their thin bodies in one by one, I'm startled by their bony frames. Tears of despair burn my eyes. If I'd known they were starving, I'd have forced Tristan to call for them sooner.

When the kids are in their pajamas and their hair has been dried, they climb into their beds. Ellie says, "Granny says you're going to marry our daddy."

"I am."

She lies down, and I pull the covers over her and tuck them under the mattress to make them tight.

Echo asks, "Are you going to wear a pretty dress?"

"I sure hope so." I work on tucking her in. "Would you like to wear one, too? I think I need three flower girls."

She asks, "What's a flower girl?"

"You know when the bride walks down the aisle to the groom?" Three little blond heads nod, and I make a note to teach them to say yes instead. "Well, before she does, the bridesmaids walk down. But even before them, we need little fairy princesses"—I point to each one as if I have a magic wand—"to get things ready."

Eva asks, "And we get to carry flowers?"

"Yes." I move to her bed as I give them a secretive smile. "But wait until you hear the best part. You get to pluck the petals off the flowers and drop them for the bride to walk on."

Echo looks horrified while Eva and Ellie clap their hands with glee.

I ask, "Echo, what's wrong?"

"The poor flowers. Imagine if I pulled your petals off," she finishes with a frown.

I give her a serious look. "I see what you mean." I tap my chin. "What should we do instead?"

"We should give everyone a flower." Her voice rings true as if she knows all.

"That's a lovely idea." I glance over at Ellie and Eva in their beds. "What do you say, girls?"

Ellie's eyes are droopy, and she yawns while Eva says, "Okay." But she's just as tired and rolls over. I walk slowly to the door and flip off the light. I turn to gaze at the three beautiful children who will soon be my daughters. Tears fill my eyes as I realize I'm living the dream I was afraid could never be mine.

CHAPTER 37

Isabelle

I DRAG MY hand along the clothing that hangs in my closet. The textures are smooth against my fingers as I marvel at the vast array before me. Once I moved in with Luke, he gave me a debit card to use for anything I wanted. My new wardrobe is one of the benefits of a rich mate.

I pull a red shirt off a hanger and slip it over my head. The silk is high quality and drapes nicely over my body. My renewed bond with Luke has put us back into the heady zone of fresh love, and we're going out to dinner to celebrate at the same restaurant where we met. My insides tremble a bit at the memory of his hand between my legs that first night, and I search for a short skirt to replace the black pants I had originally picked.

I let the slacks slither down my legs and bend over to retrieve them from the floor. Luke lets out a sexy growl as he approaches from the bathroom. "You keep your ass just like that, and we can forget about dinner."

When I stand up, his hands land on my hips, but I

twist away to face him and wave a finger. "Uh-uh. We'll miss our reservation."

He lets out a sigh and removes his towel from his waist to rub his hair. I take in his muscular body. Youth definitely has its advantages. As he walks toward his closet, I get a nice view of his round, hard backside, and I ask, "Speaking of sexy asses, can I make a request?"

I wiggle into my skirt and drag my thong down my legs to step out of it. The fabric is warm and damp in my hand as I wad it up and toss it at Luke. "No underwear for either of us."

My mate waggles his eyebrows. "You are such a naughty girl."

I slide my hands down my hips seductively. "And you're a naughty boy."

"You have no idea. You've inspired me."

I slip a foot slowly into a red stiletto heel. "I can't wait to find out."

Luke licks his lips as he watches me. I saunter over to him and notice beads of moisture on his chest from his shower. I lean down and lick him with my tongue up toward his neck to capture them. He grabs my bottom and grips tightly, so I ask, "Are you going to be the appetizer, main course, or dessert?"

He answers me with a searing kiss that says he's all three. When he's done, he says, "Stop distracting me."

I chuckle as I walk away.

When we're finally in his BMW, on our way to the restaurant, I gaze out at the sunset that turns the sky bright orange. This time of year back home, the sun never goes down. I'm growing accustomed to more evenly spaced nights and days. I wonder if it will help my mother's sleep patterns. Guilt niggles at me, because I haven't contacted Tristan to see how her arrival was. But I'm sure he'll pull me in, making it impossible to ignore Helga's presence.

Luke must be in tune with my thoughts, because he asks, "Do you plan to see your mother tomorrow?"

I glance down at my bracelet, and the silver bangle is hard in my fingers as I fiddle with it. "I know I should, but I'm not looking forward to it."

"Would you like me to come with you? My last final is in the morning." His strong arms move as he turns the wheel to steer us onto a different road.

"That's sweet." I reach over and take the hand he offers me. "But I should see her without you first."

"Tell me about her, Izzy. I want to understand."

I decide to throw him a bone. "My mother is two extremes. She can be wonderful and charm even the grouchiest bear." I smile as I remember crazy childhood adventures. "When she's happy, she's fun." We hit a pothole, and the jolt makes me hit my elbow on the door. I wince at the pain. "But when she's mad…" When I don't continue, Luke doesn't push.

He may think he understands, but he has no idea, and I don't know how to give him a taste without opening up more emotions than I'd like to deal with tonight. "Have you decided what you're going to do this summer?"

He sighs. "My dad's really pushing me to work for him, but that means I'll be inside all day."

Luke's father is a lawyer, and my mate is being groomed to become a partner when he eventually graduates from law school. Luke has never had a summer job, and he's balking at the idea that he doesn't get to play. I glance over at my man-child, and a pang of longing for a carefree life hits me. The past few months of not worrying how I was going to eat have been glorious, and I don't want them to end.

I squeeze his hand and let go to place my palm on his thigh. "If you end up having to go to the law office, you should know that a man in a suit works for me." I move my fingers up closer to his lap. "Especially when he goes commando."

Luke grabs my hand and places it over his large fabric-covered dick. "Don't make me pull over."

I growl and snap at him so he will.

Our little pit stop makes us late for the reservation, but one charming smile from Luke is all it takes to smooth things over with the hostess. She takes us to a table in the back corner, and I grin when I realize how private it is. Potted plants stand almost six feet tall and block off the space so that one has to be almost upon us to see what we're doing. My mate did indeed have plans for tonight.

Once we're seated and the waiter has taken our drink order, Luke says, "I know you tried to avoid this earlier, but I think you need to talk to me about your mother."

"Luke, it's a complicated situation."

He strokes my cheek with his finger, and I lean into his touch. "Tell me about it. My parents aren't true mates, and I'm not even sure they like each other."

"Really?"

Two vodka martinis arrive, and we sit back to let the server set them down. I lift mine as Luke says, "And to make matters worse, a little over a year ago, we found out that my mother had a child with a human before she married my father."

I gulp my mouthful of alcohol. "Oh my god." I recall that Carly is related to Luke. "Wait. Is it—"

"Carly Le Roux. All this time I had a big sister and didn't even know." He takes a sip of his drink.

"So she was raised as a human?" I shudder, imagining what it would be like to live with only people.

"Yes. She was changed by her true mate."

This is interesting. I didn't know that Carly was a new werebear. Heck, I didn't know a half-breed could even become a werebear. But what's even more interesting is that my golden-boy mate has a family with baggage. "Wow. I had no idea."

"So tell me about your parents. What is it about them that gives you those nightmares?"

I trace the edge of my martini glass with my finger, and a memory of my father flashes. Vodka was his drink of choice, and I recall the way he would hold up a glass of liquid to the darkness outside as if he were cursing it. Then he'd drink it down at once. I don't look at Luke when I say, "My father was an alcoholic. A mean one."

Luke knows my father is dead. He flips my arm over and traces a long scar on the underside of my arm as if he knows who inflicted it. I turn to him, but tears fill my eyes, and I swallow hard as I look away.

"Is he the one who causes the nightmares?"

I shake my head. My bad dreams aren't just about my past. They're also about my fear of the future. "No." I take a deep breath and turn back to face Luke. I scoot to the edge of my chair and lean in to whisper in Luke's ear. "So about that appetizer. I'm craving something salty."

I slither out of my seat and under the table. The grind of my mate's zipper tells me he's on board with my plan, and I cast away all thoughts of my family as I focus on making the man who loves me happy.

CHAPTER 38

Annie

I T'S LATE WHEN Tristan and his mother get back from their run. I was worried at first, but when I inquired, my mate assured me all was well. Helga comes in from the mudroom and drops down to a kitchen chair with a sigh. "That was interesting. I've never had to pick my way through the forest. I'm used to wide-open spaces."

"I'll bet. Did Tristan take you to the river?"

"Yes. Your water is so warm, though. I can't believe it's only going to get hotter." She fans herself with a hand. "How ever do you stay cool all summer long?"

"Air conditioning. Believe it or not, people come to Maine in the summer to vacation because it's even hotter in the southern states."

Tristan enters the kitchen and asks, "Shall I make tea?"

Helga and I nod at him as she continues speaking, "Heavens. I'm grateful the Northeast Kingdom welcomed us."

The teakettle bangs as Tristan sets it on the burner.

Helga turns to him. "Can you imagine if we'd taken the Southern Cross Kingdom up on their offer?"

He smiles at her and then glances at me. "I'd never have met my Annie. I can't imagine it at all."

I gaze at him and try to remember life before we met. "Me, either." I get up from the table to gather the selection of teas I have in the pantry. Tristan catches me by my waist as I walk by and pulls me close to give me a quick kiss. I'm touched by the tender gesture in front of his mother.

She says, "I noticed all those plants in pots you have everywhere. Tristan tells me you have quite the eye for gardening."

I bring a basket of tea bags over and sit across from her. "I love my gardens and spend too many hours in them half of the year. And then too much time designing and redesigning them the other half."

Tea bags rustle as Helga sifts through them.

Tristan says, "She's not kidding. There's an entire sketchbook dedicated to them. Every plant out there already has a place. I'll bet Annie even has the diagrams color coded so nobody could possibly get it wrong."

"I'd love to say that's not true, but it is." I grin at Helga. "I'm a bit of a control freak, but I'm learning to compromise."

"Yes, I suppose Tristan is quite the challenge." She winks at me. "So can I see your layout? I'm excited to live somewhere that I can enjoy flowers."

"Of course. I'll go get it."

This is going much better than I could have hoped for. I find my book in the great room, and the cover of it is rigid against my belly as I tuck it under my arm and return to the kitchen. Tristan is setting up the tea. Once he brings it to the table, he walks over to the cupboard, and dishes rattle as he pulls some down.

The aroma of my nighttime jasmine blend floats toward me, and I take a sip. My mate even put in the right amount of honey. Tristan sits next to me, and he sets down small plates with pieces of leftover cake. I communicate with him, *"You take good care of me."*

"That's because I appreciate you. Can you tell my mother loves you, too?"

"She's lovely. I'm not sure what you were afraid of."

I glance at Tristan, and his mouth is a tight line. He averts his gaze and still doesn't explain what is so awful about the pleasant woman sitting across from me.

I share the charts with Helga, and when she asks about how to plant things in the ground, Tristan pulls up an online video. She says, "My gosh, I hope you'll let me help you with this project."

"I'd love your help. We can do it tomorrow if you'd like."

"Do you have enough tools?"

Tristan answers her, "There's an entire section of the garage devoted to tools. If we don't have it, you don't need it."

"Wonderful." Skin rasps as Helga rubs her hands together. "I can't wait to dig into the dirt."

A yawn escapes me, and I cover my mouth, trying to hide it.

Tristan says, "It's late, Mom, and Annie and I have a busy day tomorrow."

"Oh, so it is. Well, let me clean this up for you when I'm done. I must be on arctic time, because I'm wide awake." She speaks to me, and I gaze into the crystal-blue eyes that are like Tristan's. "Would you mind if I looked through your design book?"

"Not at all. I'm always excited to share gardening with like-minded people."

Helga reaches out to me. "We're going to get along well, my dear."

I take her hand. "I think so, too. It's been so nice getting to know you, Helga."

Tristan leans down and kisses her on the cheek. "Goodnight, Mom." His voice is stern when he asks, "You will go to bed, won't you?"

She huffs, "Don't be silly. Of course I will."

I frown, wondering why he'd ask such a thing. My mate takes my hand as we make our way up the stairs. When we're in our room, I say, "I keep waiting for the difficult woman you expected. But from where I sit, your mother is a treasure."

"You're seeing the best of her. When she's like this, it's hard to believe she's crazy." A drawer thuds open, and he pulls out a pair of boxers.

I shake my head at his dramatic words and step out of my pants. The soft cotton of an oversized T-shirt slithers over my body when I put it on. Tristan goes to the bathroom. When I get there, mint wafts up to me as he hands me my toothbrush prepared with paste. Water rushes as we brush and perform our nightly rituals together.

When I begin to untangle my hair, Tristan steps behind me. His fingers flirt with the hem of my shirt, and he leans down to nibble on my shoulder. "We have a house full of people now."

I recall an incident in the room adjacent to the kitchen where people were eating lunch. "That didn't stop you when we were at my brother's." Fortunately, children don't get their heightened senses until puberty, when they come into werebear ways, and we can hide our lovemaking sounds from the girls.

One of his hands moves between my legs, and I widen my stance as I lean back. He says, "Yes, but I wasn't in the same house with my mother and children."

I inhale sharply when he strokes me. "Right."

He inserts two fingers into me, and my hairbrush clatters on the counter when I drop it to brace myself with my palms. The granite is cold under my hands, and I arch my hips back.

"Oh, love, you're offering me just what I want." Tristan presses his hard thickness against my bottom, and I squirm a bit. He shifts behind me as he removes his underwear with one hand. I gasp when he removes his fingers from me and yanks mine down. And I clasp a hand over my mouth when a yelp escapes in reaction to his teeth nipping at my backside.

Tristan lifts my shirt over my head and then presses on my back so I'll bend over the sink again. I'm rewarded with his fingers stroking me as he places his cock against my butt. The silky smoothness of him is hot against my skin.

"You're so quick to be ready for me," he says. "Think we can do this without drawing too much attention to ourselves?"

My breathing has quickened, and I pant out, "Let's try."

He drags the tip of his dick along my folds, and I long for him inside me. I rock my hips in reaction. "Please, Tristan. I'm ready."

My mate says, "I don't think so. I want you trembling with an orgasm first."

He turns me around and lifts me up to sit beside the sink. Tristan gets on his knees and places my legs over his shoulders, which allows me to grip him with my feet. He swipes his tongue over my clit and shoots pleasure through me. "Oh, God."

His chuckle vibrates against my sensitive flesh. "My mother's going to think you're religious."

I wince and try to remember to whisper instead of crying out. But with her werebear hearing, she'd have to be dead to not hear even the smallest of the sounds of our coupling. It's one of the drawbacks of the werebear world, and I put her out of my mind as something more important takes over when Tristan's tongue enters me.

My head falls back as I moan softly. I'm not able to discern what he does next because sparks of light flash behind my closed eyelids as I shatter. Still in a state of delirium, I barely notice when Tristan moves my body back into the original position of me bent over the counter. He thrusts into me before I've had a chance to come down completely, and his breath is hot on my back when he pounds into me. My core flexes around him as I climb again, and his low growl builds in volume as he gets closer.

Our flesh slaps together in our frantic movements, and his fingers dig into my hips as he tries to fill me completely. This time, I can't stay quiet, and I bury my mouth in my arm as my scream explodes. Tristan follows me and tries to hide his cries in my neck.

We pant in recovery for a moment before my mate lifts himself off me. I stand and turn to him to say, "I don't think we hid a thing."

"No. I suppose not." He rolls up my shirt to slip it over my head. The softness of the cotton is followed by my mate's hand as he caresses my breast. "I can't control myself around you, Annie. My love for you scares me."

His stubbly face scrapes against my hand as I stroke his cheek. "I know. You make life worth living."

"Hold on to that, my love. Because we're about to travel a bumpy road."

I snake my hand around his neck and stand on my tiptoes to kiss him. Before I do, I say, "I won't ever let go."

CHAPTER 39

Lucy

Tori thinks she's hiding her major crush on Keith from me, but she's so transparent. I heard he came to her presentation, and when I asked her if she was going to the ocean to wait tables with her sisters this summer, she avoided the question. I had hoped I could join her and get out of town for a while. But I bet she plans to work at the lumber mill to be near Keith.

A client of Sierra's walks through the door of Ink It, and I paste on my receptionist smile. "Hi, Pete. She'll be out for you in a few minutes."

"Great." The human sits and pulls out his phone just as Carly and her customer approach the desk. I take the girl's credit card as Carly walks over to the drink station. The machine whirs, and I hide my smile as the customer checks out the guy on the couch. The scent of her arousal gives her away—to me. The clueless human male doesn't even know she's in the room as he texts madly on his phone.

When I'm done, I head over to Carly. "Hey, so Tori

hasn't given up on Keith. I thought you should know."

Carly's spoon clinks against her coffee cup. "I figured she wouldn't. I'm not sure there's much we can do. They'll just have to work it out."

"So the call is that strong, huh?" A ceramic mug is cool in my hand as I take it from the shelf.

Carly nods as she takes a sip of her drink.

I frown, trying to imagine it. "So you start having dreams about some guy and then a burning desire to get a tattoo. Then when you get it, things become worse."

"Yes. That's why Tori can't shake her feelings. They're supposed to be so strong that she'd want to come here to be with the guy." She grins at me. "Some of us even came all the way from California."

Steam rises from my cup as I pour myself coffee, too. More than a year ago, Carly and Sierra drove here and discovered they were both from werebear descent. I smile, recalling the story I was told about how Carly tried to shoot Keith the first time he shifted for them. I wonder how Tori will react when she finds out she's part werebear, lives with one, and has even fallen for one.

I also wonder if her sisters are having the dreams, too. I say, "Tori is a triplet. Did you know that?"

Cerulean-blue eyes like mine widen on Carly's face. "No. Where are they? Do they ever come to visit?" She chuckles at herself as soon as she says the words. "Sorry. I sound like my mother-in-law, ready to play matchmaker."

I get it, though. The Le Roux are cursed with infertility, and they need the half-breed women to create the next generation. "Most of your men are kind of old now, aren't they?"

Carly shrugs. "I suppose to an eighteen-year-old they are. But Brady and I are about five years apart. It doesn't matter."

"I guess." An idea begins to blossom in my head. Maybe I should go work with Tori's sisters even if she doesn't go. I could be a half-breed liaison of sorts—and get the hell out of here for the summer.

One of the reasons I don't want to stay here approaches us. Isabelle's dressed in only a short pair of workout pants and a sports bra, showing off her immense but powerful body. Her sweaty scent turns my stomach, and I hold back my groan.

She says, "Hey, girls. What's happening in the world of tattoos?"

She does that thing with her fingers fluttering over her neck so I'll see the fresh scar of her mate bond with Luke. I roll my eyes and don't care if she sees.

Because of Isabelle, my time with my brother is non-existent. Whenever I was sick of dorm life, I'd go crash at his place for a few days. I haven't been there since Isabelle moved in, and I miss it. I used to have a posh apartment, too, but my punishment for almost flunking out of school was to live on campus, where I would be closer to classes and the library.

Carly says, "Not much. How's the world of rock-hard abs?"

Isabelle flexes her stomach and pats it. "Pretty good."

Ian is walking toward us, and he winks at me when I catch his eye. He turns to Isabelle. "Not good enough. Break time's over."

He returns his gaze to me and scans my body quickly as he says, "I'll see you tomorrow, right?"

"You sure will." I fight the flush that's rising to my cheeks.

When he turns away, Carly hits my arm lightly. "Seems someone else has a thing for older men, after all."

Now my blush heats my cheeks. "Yeah, but it won't do much good. He's not into me."

"From what I know about Ian, he might be. Maybe you need to make the first move."

The hard part about werebear romances is that a true mate could come along and ruin everything. And now that the Northeast Kingdom clans have changed the laws about interclan relationships to allow them, that likelihood is much greater. It would be just my luck to get involved with Ian and have him drop me in an instant for the real thing.

The bell over the door of Ink It jingles, and I hurry over to my desk to greet the customer. A werebear I've never seen before is glancing around, and he smiles when he sees me. He inhales deeply. "Good. I've come to the right place."

"How can I help you?" The man is on the slender side and sports tattered jeans and sneakers as if he's working the skater-dude look. His long hair is super blond, like a surfer's, and his short beard makes me think he might be my new type, because this guy's hot.

"I'm looking for Carly Cutler."

She's come up behind me and answers, "Right here. Are you a De Rozier?"

He nods, and understanding washes over me. He's from Isabelle's clan. *Well, hello there.* Because if he's a taste of the rest of them, I've got a new box of man chocolates to sample.

Carly's chuckle sounds in my head, because I forgot to block my internal dialogue. She says, "You're not supposed to be here for another two hours, but that's not a problem."

He rakes a hand through his hair. "Yeah, I caught an earlier bus."

Carly turns to me. "This is Lucy, my sister." I hold up my hand in a static wave as she continues. "I've got a client who's about to arrive, but Lucy can take you to lunch while you wait for me to be done."

The guy grins at me and sticks out his hand. "I'm Sven." I blink as I gaze into eyes so pale they're barely blue.

"Lucy." Oh, god. I'm an idiot. "But you know that."

I turn to Carly, and she hands me money as she says, "Go. I can check my appointment in."

As I walk out from behind the counter, I gaze up at the impossibly tall Sven and ask, "Pizza or burgers? I'm buying."

"Can I have both?" He pulls the door open for me.

Gorgeous, you can have anything you want. "Sure. Follow me."

CHAPTER 40

Annie

I WAKE TO a *thwap, thwap* sound punctuated by giggles. It's coming from the kitchen, and I rub my eyes as I wonder what it could be. While I recognize the laughter is from the girls, I can't figure out what the other noise is. It stops, and a squeal of joy sounds. I bolt up out of bed so I can go downstairs to investigate.

My feet tap lightly on the wooden stairs as I jog down. The staircase leads to the front-door entryway, and I have to turn and walk through the great room to get to the kitchen. The moment I round the corner, the sight before me makes my heart stop. "What the—" White smoke floats out of the doorway, and I scurry to figure out why.

When I get there, I discover it's not smoke, because the sweet taste of confectioner's sugar enters my mouth. It's all over the counter and floor, along with other substances I don't care to figure out. Egg yolk is making a slow path down the refrigerator door to meet the shells on the tile below. Three little girls are in big trouble.

Echo wallops Ellie over the head with the sugar bag, and white powder poofs out. Her face is pure joy until she discovers me. Her smile falls quickly as she freezes in place.

Eva pops the top of a can of cooking spray and is about to push the button when I yell, "Stop right there!" I growl loudly, and all three girls stare at me with eyes so wide that it would be comical if I weren't so angry. "What do you think you're doing?"

Ellie points at Eva. "She started it."

"Really. And you think that's an excuse?" I move toward them, and they scramble under the table. They huddle together, and now their faces are filled with fear. Echo whimpers and ducks her head into Ellie's shoulder. I squat down to be eye level and reach toward them. They cower together. *What do they think I'm going to do to them?*

I pull my hand back and speak softly. "I'm not going to hurt you." Eva's face is as white as snow, and I think she might vomit.

Tristan's growl behind me makes even me jump, and I stand up quickly to block the table with my body. I speak telepathically to him. *"Please calm down. They think we're going to hurt them."*

Tristan's face falls, and his shoulders slump for a second. He speaks in a stern voice that is normal volume. "Girls, beatings don't happen in this house. Please come out from under the table."

Poor Echo is shaking, and I wrap my arms around the

girls and pull them against my body as we all face Tristan. He asks, "What have you done to Annie's kitchen?"

Eva is crying loudly as Echo's tears fall silently down her face. Ellie must be the brave one, because she says, "Granny told us to make breakfast because she was busy."

I speak silently to Tristan. *"They're cooking breakfast? They're five years old."*

Tristan asks, "Do you always make breakfast?"

"No," says Ellie. "Breakfast is too 'spensive."

My heart hurts, and I turn Ellie around to ask, "Do you know what expensive means?"

She shakes her head.

I speak softly, "Girls?"

The other two turn around to look at me.

"I think you know what you did was wrong, don't you?"

They nod, and a hiccup comes out of Eva.

I say, "This is a big mess. Are you ready to clean it up?"

They nod again, and Tristan says, "I can't hear you."

Three voices reply, "Yes."

"Come with me," I say.

I give them each a job to do, and Tristan communicates with me telepathically. *"Don't help them. Hopefully, the time it takes to clean this up will teach them a lesson."*

"I think they need a punishment, too."

Pain flickers over my mate's face. *"I guess."*

"You're a softy."

Now Tristan's face clouds over with sadness, and he

says, *"I think they've suffered enough."*

I glance over at Ellie sweeping with a broom that's too big for her, and I imagine he's talking about more than hunger. The terror on the girls' faces when I yelled makes me wonder what their upbringing has been like.

My mate has been elusive about their past, but I'm not going to let it go this time. He has some explaining to do so I understand just what I'm dealing with. When I glance over at Eva wiping the table, color outside catches my eye.

I walk over to the window in amazement. My yard has been transformed. All the gardens have been planted. "Oh my God. Tristan, look." I frown. I planned on at least eight hours to put the flowers in. He comes to stand next to me as I ask, *"How did it get done?"*

Tristan's body tenses next to me, and Helga pops out from behind a trellis. She removes her gloves and waves at us as she heads toward the house. I say, "She must have been up all night."

Tristan ignores me and watches for her to enter. He growls when my future mother-in-law strolls into the kitchen and doesn't even notice the mess. Dirt is streaked on her forehead and caked on the knees of her pants. Her eyes are lit up in excitement as if nothing's wrong. "Gardening is fun. I think I'm going to love it here."

My mate's voice scares me when he says, "Mother." He glances at the girls, who are watching the exchange. They quickly get back to work.

"Come with me." He grabs her arm and tugs her back

out through the mudroom.

I'm dying to listen to their exchange, but he must be talking to her in their heads, because I can't hear anything. I notice Echo trying to get to the egg that's above her reach, and I say, "I'll get you a stepstool, honey."

Even though the girls are giving it a good effort, I know I'll be spending hours cleaning up when they finish. I can only imagine what I'll find when I pull the fridge out from the wall. I return to the pantry to make a grocery list for replacing the supplies they depleted.

The vision of the three little girls having a food fight makes me smile. I recall doing something similar with Brady, only it involved condiments. I'm not sure how old we were, but I do remember that was the fall I learned how to chop and stack wood. I glance down at my palms as if the blisters I got then have magically reappeared.

When Tristan and his mother finally return, Helga's head is down, and she lifts it slightly to speak to me as if she's a dog that's been scolded. "Annie, please forgive me. I know your gardens bring you great pleasure, and I stole it from you."

Her submissive stance makes me uncomfortable. I say, "Apology accepted. Next time, let's do it together."

She offers me a small smile and leaves the kitchen. I assume she's going to her room. The exchange was odd for me, and I wonder if the De Roziers are more old-fashioned about hierarchy.

Tristan places his hand on my shoulder as he comes to stand behind me while I monitor the cleaning. "We need to talk."

"Yes. I think it's time you told me what I've signed up for."

He sighs. "Until today, I wasn't quite sure." Tristan turns me to face him and holds my face in his hands. His gaze moves back and forth slightly, as if he's searching for something in my eyes. "Remember I told you we're headed for a bumpy road?"

I hold on to his wrists. "Yes."

"We're on it. And it's going to get worse before it gets better."

"Remember I told you I'd hold on tight?" I squeeze his arms hard. "This is me never letting go."

Tristan kisses me as his hands move from my face to thread through my hair. Soft cotton wads up in my palms as I grip his shirt and kiss him back. *"We can handle anything as long as we're together, Tristan."*

"I hope that's true. Because I don't plan to let go, either."

The End

More By the Bear
by V. Vaughn

Called by the Bear – Book 1
Called by the Bear – Book 2
Called by the Bear – Book 3

Tempted by the Bear – Book 1
Tempted by the Bear – Book 2
Tempted by the Bear – Book 3

Rocked by the Bear – The Lindquists
Rocked by the Bear – The Vachons

Desired by the Bear – Book 1
Desired by the Bear – Book 2
Desired by the Bear – Book 3

Coming 2017
Loved by the Bear Book 1,2 & 3

V. Vaughn also writes contemporary romance as
Violet Vaughn. Learn more at www.violetvaughn.com

Made in the USA
Coppell, TX
03 September 2020

36034674R10143